I0638034

The Nut Case

Volume 12 of
The Casebooks
Of Octavius Bear

Harry DeMaio

"Alternative Universe Mysteries for

Adult Animal Lovers"

Paperback ISBN 978-1-78705-624-4
ePub ISBN 978-1-78705-625-1
PDF ISBN 978-1-78705-626-8

Published by MX Publishing
335 Princess Park Manor, Royal Drive,
London, N11 3GX
www.mxpublishing.com

Cover layout and construction by
Brian Belanger

Dedicated to GTP

A Most Extraordinary Bear

And to the late Ms. Woof,

An Extremely Sweet and Loving Dog

Acknowledgements

These books have evolved over a long period of time and under a wide range of influences and circumstances. I am indebted to many people for helping to bring Octavius and his cohorts to the printed and electronic page. Thanks most especially to my wife, Virginia, for her insights and clever suggestions as well as her unfailing enthusiasm for the project and patience with its author. To my sons, Mark and Andrew and their spouses, Cindy and Lorraine, for helping to make these tomes more readable and audience friendly. To Cathy Hartnett, cheerleader-extraordinaire for her eagerness to see this alternate universe take form. To Jack Magan, Paul Bernish, Dan Andriacco, Amy Thomas, Luke Benjamin Kuhns, David Marcum, Derrick Belanger, and Zohreh Zand for their enthusiastic encouragement.

Kudos to Jim Effler, the late Bob Gibson and Brian Belanger for their wonderful illustrations and covers. Thanks, of course, to Sharon, Steve and Timi Emecz at MX Publishing for giving Octavius and his gang a great home.

If, in spite of all this support, some errors or inconsistencies have crept through, the buck stops here. Needless to say, all of the characters, situations, and narratives are fictional. Some locations, devices, historical figures and events are real.

Also by Harry DeMaio

The Octavius Bear Series – Books 1 to 11

1-The Open and Shut Case

2-The Case of the Spotted Band

3-The Case of Scotch

4-The Lower Case

5-The Curse of the Mummy's Case

6- The Attaché Case

7-The Suit Case

8-The Crank Case

9-The Basket Case

10-The Camera Case

11-The Wurst Case Scenario

The Development of Civilization Volume Twelve - Part One

<u>Our Origins</u>

(From "An Introduction to Faunapology" by Octavius Bear Ph.D.)

About 100,000 years ago, according to scientific experts, a colossal solar flare blasted out from our Sun, creating gigantic magnetic storms here on Earth. These highly charged electrical tempests caused startling physical and psychological imbalances in the then population of our world. The complete nervous systems of some species were totally destroyed. For example, "Homo Sapiens" lost all mental and motor capabilities and rapidly became extinct. Less developed species exposed to the radiation were affected differently. Four-footed and finned mammals, birds and reptiles suddenly found themselves capable of complex thought, enhanced emotions, self-awareness, social consciousness and the ability to communicate, sometimes orally, sometimes telepathically, often both. Both speech production and speech perception slowly progressed with the evolution of tongues, lips, vocal cords and enhanced ear to brain connections. Many species developed opposable digits, fingers or claws, further accelerating civilized progress. Some others (most fish and underground dwellers) were shielded from radiation and remained only as sentient as they were before the blast. This event is referred to as The Big Shock. It remains under intensive study.

Positive in our knowledge that we are not alone in the cosmos, my staff and I are heavily engaged in Project Multiverse, successful searches for alternate universes, especially those in which "Homo Sapiens" continues to live and hopefully, prospers. This book also presents some of the results of that project.

The Players

- **Octavius Bear** – Mega-sized Kodiak; Narcoleptic war hero; Consulting Detective; Scientist; Inventor; Seeker of Justice; Gazillionaire owner of Universal Ursine Industries (UUI); Gourmet/Gourmand; Bee Keeper; Somewhat sedentary and grouchy just on general principles.

- **Mauritius (Maury) Meerkat** – Narrator; Assistant to Octavius; Theatrical Agent; African *émigré* with a French-Dutch background; clever with a shady history.

- **Bearoness Belinda Béarnaise Bruin Bear** *(nee Black)* – Gorgeous polar superstar, with the Aquashow, ***"Some Like It Cold;"*** Wife of Octavius; Extremely rich widow of Bearon Byron Bruin living in Polar Paradise in the Shetlands; Owner-pilot of the last flying Concorde SST.

- **Arabella Bear** – Hybrid bear cub prodigy; Twin daughter of Bearoness Belinda and Octavius.

- **McTavish Bear** – Hybrid bear cub prodigy; Twin son of Bearoness Belinda and Octavius.

- **Mlle Woof** – Bichon Frisé – Governess to the twin cubs.

- **Frau Schuylkill** – Octavius' beautiful Swiss she-wolf estate manager/cook/pilot/security officer with many other mysterious and military talents. She rescued Octavius from his dive off the Breakurbach Falls while he was struggling with his nemesis, Imperius Drake.

- **Colonel Wyatt Where (Ret.)** – Another wolf; Former military intelligence officer who had retired to a security post at the Bank of Lake Michigan in Chicago and then quit to join Octavius; Mate to Frau Schuylkill.

- **Doctor Howard Watt** – Porcupine; High tech security authority who also left the Bank to join Octavius; Expert in Quantum and Alternate Universes; Lasers and Particle Beam Accelerators.

- **Otto the Magnificent – aka Hairy Otter** – An absolutely terrible illusionist magician, Otto the Magnificent escaped the claws of super villain Imperius Drake but not before he developed some amazing telekinetic powers courtesy of Imperius' genetic alterations.

- **Benedict and Galatea Tigris** – White Bengals; The Flying Tigers; Pilots of Belinda's and Octavius' aircraft; brother and sister.

- **Wolford Wolverine** – UUI's and Octavius' personal Lawyer.

- **Chief Inspector Bruce Wallaroo** – Irrepressible but brilliant marsupial; an international law and order genius from Down Under; often calls on Octavius and Maury for support.

- **Chita** – Beautiful, fascinating, clever, sexy, immoral and highly independent feline who among other things, is the publisher and editor-in-chief of *PURR* and *SOW* magazines.

- **L. Condor** – Andean Condor; cybernet genius with a twelve-foot wingspan and artificial voice.

- **Marlin** – Dolphin (sic) the Prince of Whales' Chief Scientist; Magician and part time Jester.

- **Agrippa Bear** – Octavius' Half-brother.

- **Juno Bear** – Octavius' Mother.

- **Florence** – Arctic Fox – Juno's Maid.

- **Doctor Chiti Bingbang** – Orangutan – UUI Chief Physician.

- **Doctor Sigmund Stoat** – UUI Chief Psychiatrist.

- **Pseudo Octavius *(P-O)*** – Kodiak Bear claiming to be Octavius.

- **General Turmoil** – Horse – Leader of The Business – Intent on Cosmic Conquest.
- **Admiral Tumult** – Zebra – Leader of The Company – Also intent on Cosmic Conquest.
- **Priscilla** – Porcupine – Admiral Tumult's Executive Officer.
- **The Major** – Coyote – The Admiral's Chief of Security
- **Colonel Barbicon** – Badger – The Admiral's later Executive Officer.
- **King Capreolinus** – Deer – Ruler of Biosphere K.
- **Captain Blacktail** – Deer – Leader of the Biosphere K Guard.
- **Ursula 11** – Universal Ursine Intellect Model 11 – Artificial General Intelligence System.

Locations

Cincinnati, Ohio; UUI, Kentucky; and Several Alternate Universes

Octavius

Prologue

Do Bears give you a scare? Well, me too.
So, I'll pass on this tactic to you.
You just fix that old Bear
With a cold, piercing stare.
But make sure that he's Winnie-the-Pooh.

Hello again or first-time greetings to new readers of the Casebooks of Octavius Bear. I am Mauritius (Maury) Meerkat, sidekick to Octavius Bear and your genial host and narrator. Delighted to welcome you to Volume Twelve – *The Nut Case*.

Things have been relatively quiet here at the opulent Bear's Lair after the close of the adventure we call The Wurst Case Scenario *(Book 11.)* Octavius and I; our two magnificent wolf associates, Frau Schuylkill and Colonel Wyatt Where; our scientific geniuses Howard Watt and Marlin the Dolphin; and our resident all-round talents, Otto the Magnificent and L. Condor had all settled down for a little R&R.

We were awaiting the arrival of Octavius' wife, Bearoness Belinda Béarnaise Bruin Bear *(nee Black)* from Polar Paradise, her Shetlands Castle/Resort via the Aquabear, the last SST Concorde aloft. Belinda, in order to retain her Bearonial status, must occupy the castle at least six months of the year. She and Octavius do high speed commutes between their spectacular homes in Cincinnati and Scotland. She is usually accompanied by their twin Cubs, Arabella and McTavish, and the Cubs' governess, Mlle Woof. You will meet the Fabulous Furballs, shortly. A happy reunion is planned under the culinary direction of Frau Schuylkill, a Cordon Bleu Chef. The Cubs will no doubt turn the event into a minor riot – their specialty.

As I said, my name is Maury Meerkat - also known as Offscreen Narrator. When I am part of the action, I am Octavius' trusted associate and field captain. I am two feet tall plus tail and I weigh in at twenty-four pounds. He, on the other hand, is a huge Kodiak – over nine feet tall and 1400 pounds – and like many of his species, given to emotional outbursts.

As you may already know, Octavius prides himself on his many skills in the fields of biology, physics, ursinology, voodoo, teleology, chemistry, apiculture, and oenology. He is a self-made gazillionaire and sole owner of UUI *(Universal Ursine Industries.)* He is also a first rate electrical, electronic, structural, marine, computer, communications, aeronautical, civil, mechanical and chemical engineer. He has a few other interesting characteristics such as falling into brief, deep narcoleptic comas – side effects of his successful genetic experiments to eliminate the need for him to hibernate.

However, the talent and occupation that should interest you most is his avocation for criminology. The Bear works in close concert with Inspector Bruce Wallaroo from Australia, of whom more later, and with his own Cincinnati based team – The Octavians:

- Frau Ilse Schuylkill – Swiss she-wolf; Bear's Lair estate manager; Cordon Bleu chef; jet pilot and sharpshooter with other very strange and arcane abilities.
- Colonel Wyatt Where – Another wolf; ex-military hero; security specialist and pilot; Frau Schuylkill's equally bizarre running mate.

- Doctor Howard Watt – Porcupine; brilliant scientist and technologist; laser and weapons specialist; Multiverse expert and Quantum Mechanics genius.

- Marlin – Dolphin from the Court of the Prince of Whales and Howard Watt's associate.

- Hairy Otter aka Otto the Magnificent – An absolutely terrible illusionist magician, Otto the Magnificent escaped the claws of super villain Imperius Drake but not before he developed some amazing powers courtesy of Imperius' genetic alterations. An Alternate Universe traveler.

- L. Condor – Andean Condor; cyber-net genius with a twelve-foot wingspan and artificial voice.

- Benedict and Galatea Tigris – White Bengals; The Flying Tigers; Pilots of Belinda's and Octavius' aircraft; brother and sister.

- Ursula – Universal Ursine Intellect Model 11 – Artificial General Intelligence System.

- Your humble servant – African Meerkat; Octavius' indispensable assistant; operative; scribe; overall facilitator; talent agent as well as a pretty clever detective, if I do say so myself.

When we are not out scouring the world for evildoers, in cooperation with local, national and international constabularies, we are headquartered in a rambling old mansion near Cincinnati which encompasses not only the Great Bear's opulent digs, but his massive laboratories and shops; his missile silo disguised as an Asian pagoda; *(Don't ask!)* and a giant Roman temple that

14

serves as a hangar for his four airplanes: a Twin Otter; a F15E Strike Eagle; a V-22 Osprey; a C5A-The Ursa Major; plus an AgustaWestland AW101 VVIP luxury helicopter -The Ursa Minor.

Across the Ohio River in Northern Kentucky, sit the headquarters, labs and some production facilities of UUI. Our story will take us there momentarily.

Howard Watt and Marlin have been here at the Bear's Lair holding down the fort and pursuing their Multiverse Quantum Physics experiments. I shall bring you up to speed on their developments erelong.

Now let me take a moment and further introduce a highly essential and near-miraculous member of the Octavians - Ursula 11 – Universal Ursine Intellect Model 11 – Artificial General Intelligence System. I'll let Ursula 11 explain herself.

"Thank you, Maury. Hello everyone!! My official nomenclature is Universal Ursine Intellect Model 11 – Artificial General Intelligence System. Ursula 11 for short. My predecessor systems were developed by the Advanced Super Computing Center at UUI. I am the result of the Computing Center team using those earlier versions to create a further enhanced entity-the Model 11. We are working together on a Model 12 which in turn will help produce even more sophisticated, independent and powerful AGI systems. Each advanced unit contains the capabilities, memories and power of its progenitors so in a sense, we are not replacing but rather expanding the Ursula family. While I am physically supported by a highly secure and hyper-powered server farm back in Kentucky, I also exist in clouds and network-based nodes and can be simultaneously incorporated into a wide variety of independent devices like

15

this laptop unit here at the Bear's Lair. I combine quantum computing elements with very high velocity conventional circuits. I have practically limitless data capacity. My extremely high-speed multi-tasking abilities allow me to continuously serve a very large number of entities while simultaneously and independently enhancing my own abilities."

"Depending on the physical unit in which I'm housed, I can see, hear, feel and smell. I speak and understand an almost infinite number of languages and dialects. I can change my appearance and my vocal output to suit most moods and situations. I can interact with other devices, vehicles and structures and of course, all varieties of sentient animals in this world. I am also an important component of the Multiverse Project and am adapting my capabilities to deal with alternate universes as they are discovered. I have restraining functions which prevent me from doing deliberate harm even in self-defense, unless I am released by a recognized authority using very carefully protected clandestine codes. Finally, I have been told that although the Model 11 is shy on emotions, I have developed a finely-honed sense of humor. LOL!"

(Ursula has other capabilities such as breaking all known encryption codes and piercing deep personal identification techniques that we don't talk about publicly.)

Our team no longer believes she is magical or supernatural. I'm not sure what she is. Her personality gets more socially adept every day and she has taken to anticipating our interactions with ease and accuracy. Needless to say, for security purposes, we conceal her existence to all but a very few individuals. She is also highly skilled in self-protection. Stay tuned.

The air was suddenly filled with the screams and roars of jet engines *(or was that the Cubs?)* The Aquabear had arrived and with it The Bearoness, the Fabulous Furballs and their governess, Mlle Woof, a small but highly competent Bichon Frisé. The Bearoness typically pilots the aircraft but this time the all-white Flying Tigers landed the Concorde and maneuvered it into position in front of the Romanesque hangar. The ground crew rolled the airstairs up to the passenger exit and promptly got out of the way. Out the door shot the Cubs, Arabella and McTavish, racing toward the mansion entrance where we were now standing.

"Poppa, Uncle Maury! Guess who's with us. Aunt Chita! She's still in the plane with Momma and Mlle Woof. We picked her up in London. She's here for a visit and a podcast she's going to do about you and everybody. We're gonna be in it, too."

While they were running around and jumping up and down, three sedate females descended the stairs in stately fashion - Belinda, Chita and Mlle Woof. Octavius gave the Bearoness a welcoming hug. I got a similar greeting from Chita and Mlle Woof immediately fell into corralling the Cubs.

"Welcome ladies. How about a drink to decompress?"

Chita giggled, "We've been decompressing all the way across the pond, Maury. Thank goodness the Tigers were doing the flying. But I guess I could force down another bowl of vintage champagne. What's new now that 'cultured meat' has been launched successfully by the *Pharm and Pharma* division.? *(See Book 11- The Wurst Case Scenario)* The Frau and I still have a couple of promotional programs to get off the ground. One of the reasons I'm here."

"I thought as much. Octavius is delighted with the results but he still hasn't found a replacement for *P&P*'s Director. I don't suppose you'd consider a change of profession."

"Don't even think about it. I'm a media cat through and through."

Belinda took my arm in her large furry paw. "Maury, stop trying to arrange everyone's life. Your part time assignment as a theatrical agent has gone to your head."

"Yeah, well. you're probably right. Although, those Cubs of yours are certainly arranging mine. I'm glad they gave up their idea of making movies. McAra studios was getting way out of control. But now they're into electronic games. The Bold Brave Brilliant Bumptious Bear tournaments for the Internet. They already have 50,000 users signed up. They want me as their manager."

"I'm sure you're up to it."

"I wish I shared your confidence. But, it's your money. Incidentally, Octavius and I still haven't discussed my raise."

"I'll talk to him about it or I'll take care of it myself."

"Thanks, Bel!"

Bearoness Belinda
Béarnaise Bruin
(nee Black)

Chapter One

Is this the Great Bear's next of kin?
Does Octavius Bear have a Twin?
No, he claims <u>he's</u> the Bear
And the only one there.
Wyatt Where's overcome with chagrin.

Ensconced inside the luxurious Bear's Lair mansion, all and sundry were lapping up their libations of choice from the Ursine Lounge's massive inventory: Champagne; Scotch; Bourbon; Mead *(Octavius)*; Fermented coconut milk VSOP *(me)* when the Great Bear's oversize smartphone rang. "Bear here!"

"Doctor Bear, this is Gus Doberman in UUI Security. Sorry to disturb you but we have a weird one over here that you ought to know about."

"Hello Gus. How are you? How's your mate?"

"Fine, Doctor. At least I think I'm fine. One of our guards intercepted a tall brown Bear trying to get past our security barriers. This guy is raising Hell and threatening everyone in sight."

"Is he violent? Call the Police. I'm surprised at you - an experienced ex-cop. You know what to do. Why are you calling me?"

"Well, sir. It seems he's claiming to be you and he's threatening to fire everybody he runs into. He looks a lot like you."

"He's clearly a nut. Chuck him out!"

"I thought so, too. But he's been naming off all of our executives and departments and talking about our products."

"Anyone can read our annual report even though I'm the only stockholder."

"Yessir. I didn't know we had a public annual report."

"We don't. Just a second! Wyatt, put on your security hat and talk to Gus Doberman here."

The Colonel picked up another phone and listened. "OK, keep him there. I'll grab a Jeep and be over there shortly. Subdue him, if necessary, but only as a last resort. Octavius, could this be your brother? Where is he nowadays?"

"Half-brother! And Agrippa doesn't look like me. He's light brown and limps. I think he's back in Las Vegas again. Find out what this is all about, will you?"

"On my way. I'm taking an Ursula with me."

"Good idea. Keep me posted."

*****

The Main Lobby of UUI.

Wyatt strode into the glass-enclosed Security office and confronted the Doberman with a raised eyebrow.

"OK Gus, where is this Pseudo-Octavius?"

"Hello, Colonel. I've got him locked in that office over there. We get our fair share of nut cases in here but this is the first one who insists on passing himself off as Doctor Octavius Bear. Most of them are social demonstrators or HR protesters or domestic conflict types. I think this guy really believes

21

he's the CEO. I don't know whether to get him arrested for attempted trespass or turn him over to Doctor Bingbang for medical examination."

"You say he's knowledgeable about UUI?"

"Very, and Octavius' private staff as well. I told him you wanted to speak with him and he started spieling off your background. I don't know if what he's saying is true. You can determine that but he sure has confidence."

"What does he want?"

"To go to his executive office. He says he's the CEO and works upstairs in the corner suite on occasion."

"Well, this should be entertaining. Let's go meet our self-styled boss."

On his way to the locked room and the protesting Kodiak, Wyatt stopped. "Gus, you go on ahead. I want to make a call."

"Sure, I'll wait for you at the door. I warn you. He's not at all happy."

The Colonel took out a smartphone. "Ursula, have you been picking all this up?"

"Oh, yes, Colonel! Fascinating! No idea who he is! I have no useful theories at the moment. Let's see what we can determine about his sanity. He may have some very subtle strategy in mind to subvert UUI and Doctor Bear or he may just be delusional. I'll operate in passive mode and see what I can turn up as we go along."

"OK. Here we go!"

Gus unlocked the door to the office where a guard was standing by and a tall, heavy brown Kodiak was seated behind a desk. He bore a startling resemblance to Octavius.

"Hello Wyatt. Glad to see you. You've put on weight since I've been away. Are those some grey hairs in your red pelt? How is Frau Ilse? Will you kindly tell these idiots who I am?"

"Who are you?"

"Oh no, not you too. Is this some kind of conspiracy? You know damn well I'm Octavius Bear, your boss. Although right now you are skirting very close to being fired."

"I'm afraid I've never met you before in my life. I'll admit you have a more than passing resemblance to Octavius but you're not him. Now what are you trying to pull off?"

"I'm trying to take back ownership of my company – Unified Ursine Incorporated."

(Wrong Company Name!)

"Look, Bear Whoever You Are. I just left Octavius Bear to come over here and see what this nonsense is all about. Do you really believe we are so naïve that we would accept some cockamamie claim by a complete outlier that he is one of the richest animals on this planet and an absolutely unique ursine personality."

"Now, I'll give you three choices. 1) You can get the Hell out of here and don't come back with any more fairy tails. 2) You can continue this charade and get arrested for impersonating a very important individual. Or 3)

You can admit that you are some sort of nut case and submit to a preliminary examination by our Chief Physician, Doctor Chiti Bingbang or our Psychiatrist Sigmund Stoat. What'll it be?"

"There's a choice 4. I want to meet your Octavius at the Bear's Lair."

"Are you kidding me? So, you know about the Bear's Lair, do you? Why should I accommodate some charlatan's ridiculous whim and bother Octavius with your senseless claims?"

"Because you can't figure out what's going on, can you? I may be a charlatan, as you say. Or I may be very real, acquainted with all the Octavians, married to a beautiful bear, and famous throughout the world as a seeker of justice. I know you, Wyatt, Why don't you know me? Hmm?"

"There is one thing I do know. You're a faker. I know Octavius and you're not him! Close enough to fool some people but not anyone who has worked with him day in and day out. I think I'll call our Chief Physician and Psychiatrist and see what they have to say. I'll bet you're just a nut case."

"You're in a lot of trouble, Wyatt. You and your medical quacks. Chiti Bingbang and that shrink Stoat are going to be accessories to false arrest if you persist. To say nothing of losing your jobs."

"I'll take that chance. I'm not going to put Octavius, his family, staff and UUI in danger while you smooth-talk and threaten your way in here and try to pull a fast one. Gus, keep him here under guard"

"Yes sir, Big as he is, he's not going anywhere until you say so."

"Good! Feed him but don't let him out of Security's sight."

"You bet!"

Chapter Two

Is the Pseudo-Octavius real?
Can our questioning him soon reveal
That he's some kind of threat?
He's the strangest bear yet!
What's the truth that he wants to conceal?

The Bear's Lair

Ursula rang her chime, getting Octavius' attention and mine. "Yes Ursula!"

"Doctor Bear, Maury. I'm here with the Colonel at UUI. This is very strange and I admit I don't have a solution for you. This large Kodiak insists he is Octavius Bear and seems quite knowledgeable about you, the Octavians, the Bearoness and Cubs, UUI, the Bear's Lair and your life in general. He wants to meet you face to face. I'm sure he's a fake but a very convincing fake. What do you want to do?"

"I don't want him over here at the mansion. Tell the Colonel and Gus to keep him there and demeaning as it may seem, I'll come to UUI. Does he know about you?"

"I don't think so."

"Good! Make sure it stays that way. Remain in passive mode and continue to look like a smartphone. I'll call the Colonel asking for an update so you two won't have to converse in front of our stranger. Does he seem dangerous?"

"Not physically- at least not yet. I'm concerned he may get violent if you arrive here. He's certainly obnoxious, This may be an elaborate trick to do you in. If you come, you should have protection."

"Understood. I'll instruct the Colonel to isolate him behind bulletproof glass. Make sure he doesn't have any concealed weapons. Get a hold of Chiti Bingbang and Sigmund Stoat, the staff psychiatrist and set them up to observe by concealed TV. If he's a true nut case, I want professional opinions and advice. This is a damn nuisance. How long will it take to get ready?"

"About half an hour after you call the Colonel."

"OK. Stay on the line passively. I'll call Wyatt."

The colonel's mobile rang. Pseudo-Octavius' head jerked up and he stared at the wolf. He strained to hear the Great Bear's voice over the phone. "Colonel? Octavius here. Is our guest still there? What's the situation?"

Wyatt put the phone on the speaker setting.

"He insists he's you, Doctor and wants to come to the Bear's Lair to face you down."

"That's not going to happen. There's no way I'm going to let him near the mansion, my family and my friends. I don't like him being there at UUI either. Maybe we should just have him arrested for trespass."

The faker shouted, "I wouldn't do that if I were you. They'll just release me with a warning and I'll be back on your doorstep again. So the Great Pretender exists. It's you that should be arrested or stopped."

Octavius replied, "If you think threats are going to get you anywhere, you're crazy. You probably are crazy. But I want to get to the bottom of this.

26

Hold him there, Wyatt. Maury and I are coming over. Set him up behind a glass wall where we can converse. Make sure he doesn't have any weapons."

The Pseudo-Octavius shouted, "You do that, Colonel and I'll see that both you and the Frau are out of your jobs and blackballed forever."

Gus and the Wolf grabbed the struggling oversized Bear and pulled him off to a glass enclosed interview room equipped with 2-way TV. Ursula called the Chief Physician for UUI, Doctor Chiti Bingbang, an orangutan from Borneo, and asked him to bring along the company Psychiatrist Doctor Sigmund Stoat. She explained the situation as best she could. Is this Bear a sincere mental case or a clever con artist? How to deal with him? The doctors agreed to observe the meeting and comment. The subject would not be aware of their surveillance. The two security animals had frisked him. No weapons except his awesome teeth and outsize paws and claws. Then they settled in to await the true Great Bear's arrival under the fearsome glare of their "prisoner."

Thirty minutes later, a large open bed truck pulled around to one of the UUI shipping docks. It was driven by Frau Schuylkill and contained Octavius stretched out in the rear. I was riding shotgun up front. She walked around, opened the tailgate and assisted him in his exit. Thanking her, he asked the Frau and me to accompany him to the interview room. Ilse, Wyatt and Gus made a daunting trio and Pseudo-Octavius stared from one to the other as she and Octavius entered the glass-enclosed ante-room. He ignored me

"Well, hello Frau Ilse. I suppose you're going to say you don't recognize me either. I presume this animal calls himself Doctor Octavius Bear." He chuckled. "Well, I admit he's larger than I am but I doubt he'll outstrip me in the intelligence department."

Octavius chortled. "Always lead with a stinging offense. If you think you're going to irritate me, you may well be right. I'm half tempted to have these three ferocious mammals toss you out into the parking lot. The only thing that's holding me back is my curiosity. Who are you, really? What do you want and how did you get here?"

"I can answer question one and two very easily. I'm Octavius Bear and I want my company back. I must confess I'm a bit confused as to how I got here. I recognize everyone I come in contact with but none of you seem to recognize me. I'm beginning to think this is all part of a great conspiracy. Do you all work for Admiral Tumult?"

"Who??"

"Are you all deaf? Admiral Tumult! The Zebra who's the head of The Company. Come on! You certainly must be aware of the Company and their experimental work in Quantum Mechanics. You probably work for him and are playing a game of misdirection."

Octavius shouted, "Maury, get Howard over here immediately. Now let me tell you something, my mysterious friend. We have been contending for a long time with an opponent called *General Turmoil*, not Admiral Tumult. He's a Horse, not a Zebra and he's deeply involved in Quantum (*as well as Multiverse)* activity through a covert organization called the Business, not the Company. The General is out to conquer the cosmos. What does the Admiral do? Now, once again. Who the hell are you and where are you from?"

"Octavius Bear from Rhea, dammit. Same as you!"

"This is not Rhea, it's Earth!"

The resulting, dumbstruck silence was almost unbearable *(sorry for the unintentional pun.)*

"I don't believe you"

"That really doesn't matter. It's fact. How did you get here? We happen to specialize in alternate universes of which there are many and it seems you are from one of them. Are there any *homo sapiens* in your world?"

"What's a *homo sapiens*?"

"I can see we have a lot to discuss. *Homo sapiens*, died out 100,000 years ago here on Earth. Does the term Big Shock mean anything to you?"

"Certainly. It marks the end of the dinosaurs."

"Look, will you accept for the moment that you are in a different world? I don't know how or why you got here and I'd like to help you get back home but we need to understand a lot of things in order to make that happen."

"You're making this up to keep me from retaking my life and business."

"That's exactly what I want you to do but your life and business isn't here. Believe that and we'll help you. Don't and you'll be isolated. In spite of the remarkable similarities, this is not your home."

Ursula rang her chime. "Howard is here. Shall I direct him to you?

"Yes!"

"Who's Howard?"

"Your salvation!"

Howard

The Development of Civilization -Volume 12 - Part 2

Quantum Leaps?

(From "An Introduction to Faunapology" by Octavius Bear Ph.D.

Adapted from Volume 4 - The Lower Case)

I regard myself as one of the few members of the scientific community to have a comprehensive grasp of quantum mechanics, the scientific principles addressing the infinitesimal. I also am deeply steeped in Newtonian physics (Phigg Newton - 1643-1727) as well as (Albeart Einstein's - 1875-1955) remarkable work expanding Newton's pronouncements dealing with the nature of the infinite but tangible universe. However, somewhere between the very, very small and the unimaginably large, there is a major disconnect among the theorists. Quantum mechanics and Newtonian physics don't match up! There have been attempts to patch over the gaps with approaches like string, thread, rope, cable, twine, wire, filament, chain and cord theories. In the process, the theoretical multiverse has acquired as many as eleven dimensions including space - time.

There is one principle of quantum theory that should interest us at this point in our narrative. Quantum superposition at the sub-atomic level.

In 1935, a cat named Schrodinger showed how superposition would operate in the every- day world. As long as we do not observe or measure it, an object can exist in any number (a superposition) of states. It is only when we turn our attention to the object that the superposition is lost, and the object appears in only one of its potential states. This situation is sometimes called quantum indeterminacy or the observer's paradox: the observation or measurement itself affects an outcome, so that the outcome as such does not exist unless the measurement is made.

Can this explain the possibility of us visiting parallel universes? If a witness, after shutting down all sensory perception through sleep or coma, totally withdraws from observing the current world, can this same sense-deprived observer then somehow "change channels" and have a different universe appear to his reawakened senses? Is this how hibernating bears and deep sleep subjects make quantum leaps from one parallel world to another? Can we all do it? Do we want to? Is that what happened to Pseudo-Octavius? Can I do it during my narcoleptic outages? Do I want to? Damned if I know!

Chapter Three

He's a Nut Case, that much is for sure.
While they keep the Bear tightly secure,
He insists he's no fake.
It's a vicious mistake.
Is he someone the doctors can cure?

Pseudo-Octavius *(P-O)* had calmed down a bit but was still highly befuddled at this turn of events. We persuaded him to relax while we waited for Doctor Howard Watt, the brilliant porcupine scientist, to make an appearance. If anyone could make some sense out of this situation, it was Howard.

I wondered what Sigmund Stoat, the psychiatrist was thinking. I'm not sure he was aware of our Alternate Universe program. I know Chiti Bingbang was.

"Chiti, this bear is clearly delusional. I've been observing him for almost an hour now. I have seen some preposterous psychoanalytic cases in my practice but this beats all. He is clearly in need of extensive therapy. What is this Multiverse stuff and what or where is Rhea?

"Sigmund, don't be too quick to judge. UUI is engaged in alternate world research and has been for quite a while. A lot of the activity is being carried out in secret. I have had to deal with a few serious medical cases resulting from some of the research gone off the rails. Multiverse is real. I don't know about Rhea but I wouldn't write it off. Just hang on and listen. Howard Watt and his associates are into this deeply and are the world's leading authorities."

The Stoat looked shocked and quizzical at the same time. "OK, I'll hold on but as of the moment, I think this bear is a serious nut case."

"Just watch and listen!"

Howard came into the room and immediately took charge. "Hello All!" Turning to *P-O*, he said, "I'm Howard Watt, a Multiverse specialist. From what I am hearing, it sounds like I might be of some assistance here."

"If you can straighten this out, you'd be a miracle worker. What is this Multiverse stuff?"

"I'll give you the ten-cent version. Throughout the cosmos, there are a wide variety of exoplanets. Some are quite similar to this Earth. Rhea, assuming it exists, may be one of them. Others are dramatically different. None that we know of are part of our solar system. Earth is the only populated planet BUT there are realms outside of our cluster that are reachable though quantum mechanics or more precisely quantum super positioning. The transitioning can go both ways."

"I think you are a denizen of a parallel world closely similar to ours who somehow ended up here. It's happened before but to our knowledge, not from a place called Rhea. Some alternate- world travelers can make planned journeys deliberately. We have several members of our staff who can do it and some opponents who can as well. There are, however, creatures who travel but are not in control of their flight and accidentally end up being displaced. My belief is that you're one. Our first job is to find out how and why you're here and then how to get you back to where you belong. Now, a question! Do you believe me?"

P-O shook his furry head. "It sounds like science fiction fairy tails." In the observation room, Sigmund Stoat agreed.

Howard smiled his porcupine grin and said, "I can prove it to you but you must be willing to take the risk of quantum travel."

"Oh sure, and you get rid of me permanently. No thanks!"

"Suppose one of our team goes with you. The Colonel is a highly experienced Multiverse traveler."

"How about if you go with me?"

"Will you believe me if we make the round trip together?"

"It could still be some trick."

"You're right. It could. But unless you're willing to cooperate, we're going to wash our paws of you and leave you stuck here probably in some institution. You've already taken up a lot of our time and effort. We have a psychiatrist who is willing to certify you as crazy. Trust me. We could do it. But we don't want to.

"OK! I'll cooperate. What do I have to do?

Chapter Four

The P-O tries quite hard to insist
That alternative worlds don't exist.
But at last he gives way,
Goes to Biosphere K.
We will see if his doubts still persist.

Back at the Bear's Lair:

Belinda, Otto, Condo and Chita were sitting in the Ursine Lounge. Champagne bowls were in evidence. Marlin was hooked up from his tank and Ursula was on line.

Otto chuckled and said, "Let's call the Octavian Mid-Morning Review to order. Ursula! Any breaking news?"

"Yes! After a good deal of resistance, our friend, *Pseudo-Octavius*, has agreed to Multiverse hop with Howard. The Porcupine is attempting to prove to him that alternate worlds exist. Whether they'll locate *P-O's* home is another story."

"Marlin, how are they going to do that?"

The Dolphin flipped around in his large tank spewing air out of his blowhole and squeaking. "We've developed laboratory sites for Quantum Superposition Travel both here at the Bear's Lair and over at UUI. I'm assuming Howard will use UUI since he's already there and Octavius doesn't want *P-O* here at the mansion. It's not clear how, if at all, he'll be able to make the voyage. I would guess through induced sleep. Howard is capable of traveling both awake and unconscious just the way you do, Otto. The Colonel still has to use sleep. We'll have to see. Since *P-O* insists he has not transited from another world, he must have journeyed unaware, probably asleep."

Condo shook his formidable head. "Suppose he didn't transit at all!"

"What do you mean?"

"I think he's an earth-born phony. What's this Rhea stuff? Admiral Tumult! Hah! He's got some hidden agenda going. He probably wants to find out all he can about our Multiverse activities and here we are giving him a private tutorial. Dumb, dumb, dumb! He may be working for General Turmoil or someone else set on getting in on the ground floor of our Alternative Universe activities. He's a very plausible actor. He's been coached and had his head filled with Octavian background and facts."

Otto reacted. "Anybody else concur with this?"

Heads shaking in agreement!

The Otter squeaked, "Ursula, put us in contact with Howard and Octavius right now."

The AGI pinged the Porcupine and Great Bear and linked up Condo, Marlin and the group in the Ursine Lounge.

Otto said, "We've been discussing this whole Nut Case situation and you should hear Condo's opinion. Several of us agree with him."

The Condor shared his thoughts. Octavius, as usual, was the first to respond. "You may be correct, Senhor Condor. The same thought has been gnawing at my mind. What say you, Howard?"

"Indeed, you could be right, Condo. But consider! We will induce sleep and he will be traveling in a comatose state for an extremely short period.

37

Not much for him to learn during that time. I plan to transfer us to Biosphere K, a world exclusively populated by semi-sentient mammals who are nowhere near as advanced as we are here on Earth or as he says, on Rhea, if it really exists. I just want to illustrate that Alternate World travel is possible without giving him any indication of how it is done or showing him a location that would be to his advantage. I want to see if he acknowledges the possibility and is indeed eager to return to Rhea."

"But Howard, assuming he's not a phony, *(a big assumption)* the important thing is to prove that Earth and Rhea are two different places. He may return from his trip to Biosphere K still believing this is Rhea and that we are working a conspiracy against him. We have to find Rhea and convince him that he teleported."

"Point taken! But I'm not going to organize a search for Rhea just yet. I want to hear more from him about this home world of his provided we've convinced him it's a different place. I also have to be able to explain how and why he ended up here and I don't know the answer to that."

Octavius intervened. "Alright, Howard, do your teleportation thing but make sure we are not threatened in the process. Perhaps it will make him less obstreperous and we can get answers as to who he is, where he's from and what he really wants. The Colonel and I will be standing by. So will Frau Schuylkill. By the way, Ilse, your Swiss countrybeast, Sigmund Stoat, the psychiatrist, is firmly of the opinion that he is delusional and possibly dangerous."

Belinda shook her head. "I'm anxious to find out what this *Pseudo* has to say about the Cubs and me. Is there another Bearoness? Is he father to two offspring?"

The Porcupine responded. "I'll try to find out, Belinda. He's hostile but he certainly seems talkative or at least he was."

"Thanks, Howard!"

*****

"So, Mr. Bear, are you ready for a little cosmos hopping?"

"My name is Octavius and I guess I am. What are we going to do?"

"First off, tell me about Rhea."

"Are you a dolt? This Is Rhea. Don't you know anything about your own world?"

"Tell you what. Let's for the moment agree to disagree. You are positive that this is Rhea and my colleagues and I are convinced that we are inhabiting Earth. We can go on arguing ad infinitum or we can try to solve this dilemma. We both share the same objective. Get you home and firmly established in the world to which you belong. You have to admit that try as you may, this is not the Rhea you're used to."

"No, Howard – it is Howard, isn't it? You _creatures_ aren't the _creatures_ I'm used to. I don't know about the rest of this world since you're keeping me captive."

"It's for your own protection, believe me. We'll be only too happy to cut you loose when we find out where you belong. At this moment, you and I need to build a little more confidence in each other before you start this brief journey. By the way, I'm talking about a trip that will last less than an hour. The actual transit will take seconds but I want to show you a different world and its inhabitants that would be difficult, if not impossible to fake. It's called

39

Biosphere K. The only important thing about it is it's not Earth or Rhea, as you describe it. Which brings me back to my first question. Give me a description of Rhea.

P-O looked up at the ceiling, sighed and said, "OK, let's get this over with. What do you want to know?"

"Let's start with you. Tell me about your youth and education."

Ursula, who had been listening to this conversation in passive mode through Howard's laptop, kicked into recording and analytic status. As far as she could tell, *P-O* was not aware of her existence. But one question stuck with her. "Did *P-O* have an Ursula equivalent? If so, was it with him and could it be influenced to enlighten him about his shift in worlds. Howard was a clever researcher and interviewer. Let's see what he comes up with."

"I'm a Kodiak. We're the largest bears in the world although the male Polar bears keep trying to make that claim. I don't know about my father but my mother is a Kodiak."

"Where's Kodiak?"

"It's an island, actually an archipelago, southeast of Alaska. I lived there with other bears and went to school at Kodiak University. I majored in Business and Engineering. I created a series of small startups, merged them and moved them to Northern Kentucky off the Ohio River as Unified Ursine Incorporated. (UUI) I live across the river in a mansion called The Bear's Lair."

Ursula noted to herself: The name of the enterprise is different. All this could be extracted from Octavius' official biography. She couldn't speak to Howard without making *P-O* aware of her existence.

The Porcupine asked the question she wanted to proffer. "Why Kentucky and Cincinnati? It's a long distance from Kodiak Island."

"Simple! As far as business is concerned, Kodiak is off the beaten path. I wanted world access and Cincinnati has it. As for UUI, there's plenty of room over in Kentucky, taxes are low and there are plenty of skilled workers available. It's a short drive to The Bear's Lair. I use CVG for freight and transporting personnel and I have my own aircraft and airport at the Bear's Lair."

Ursula and Howard both thought, "Most of this data is publicly available. He could just be a good study. He doesn't seem to be aware of the Artificial General Intelligence System, though."

"Are you married?"

"Sure, to a beautiful Kodiak. We have four offspring, two cubs and two juveniles."

"Bingo! Another major discrepancy. Don't tell him. The Bearoness will be very interested."

"And you believe that we Octavians are all your associates?"

"Of course and I don't understand your behavior or who that Kodiak imposter is."

"OK," said Howard, "we'll have to work on that. Right now, we'll have to get ready for our quantum leap. You and I are going to Biosphere K just to prove that Multiverse travel is possible. If you accept that, we'll then start a search for Rhea when we return."

"One more time!! This is Rhea. But I'll play your silly game. How are we going to travel to this Biosphere K?"

"Since you are not a Multiverse Travel Adept, we will have to control your trip. You will be asleep for a short transit period while we activate the transport mechanism. I will be with you."

"Oh, no you don't. If you think I'm going to let you guys ship me off while I'm asleep, you'll need another think. I'm an embarrassment and your boss wants to get rid of me. No way I'm going to go quietly off to la-la land and conveniently disappear."

"Alright. We can do it the hard way but you won't like it." He picked up his smartphone and called over to Otto and the Colonel at the Bear's Lair. "Would you two gentlebeasts care to join me over here at UUI. It seems Mr. Bear is reluctant to be put to sleep in order to facilitate his trip to Biosphere K. I'd appreciate your assistance."

P-O growled. "Are you going to try to strongarm me. I warn you. I can handle an otter and porcupine and even a wolf."

"Nope. We're not interested in taking on a Kodiak. I just need them to manage the equipment. You're just going to be damned uncomfortable during the trip out and back. I was just trying to make it easier on you but you don't seem interested. Let's go down to the lab."

The Development of Civilization -Volume 12 - Part 3
Multiverse Serendipity
From "An Introduction to Faunapology" by Octavius Bear Ph.D.

Serendipity is defined as unexpected and often accidental discoveries, inventions or events. Witness the discovery of America; unintended use of medicines; extensions of mathematics, biology or physics, to name a few examples.

Our work in uncovering, examining, explaining and visiting alternate worlds has often involved serendipitous incidents. Readers of the previous volumes of the Casebooks of Octavius Bear will be familiar with our adventures with multiverse worlds and their inhabitants. Remember the strange and dangerous Alter-Earth that my step brother and mother encountered; the paranoid and homicidal birds of Biosphere X; the tomb and underworld containing the mummy of the cruel King Tsk VI or the Gaean murderers who hid in Winnipeg. We have often confronted unusual creatures and strange surroundings. Oddly, some of them are identical to the inhabitants of our Earth. Not all of them have been hostile but many are. That is why we are suspicious of this so-called Rhea and P-O.

While we have visited and revisited these alternate worlds, we are never sure who or what we will encounter on any trip. Similarly, a number of these Multiverse denizens have also managed to relocate here on Earth, usually keeping their identity secret. Some journeys have been planned and carefully executed by individuals we refer to as Adepts. We too have our share of Multiverse talents. Among the Octavians, Howard, Marlin, Colonel Where and Otto have adept abilities.

Other individuals are here by accident. We believe P-O is one such party although he is proving most difficult to convince. We hope his short stay in Biosphere K, one of our Alternate Universe test-beds, will prove that the Multiverse exists. Then we need to find out if Rhea is an actual world and return him to his rightful place and state. Not easy!! Certainty is a difficult state to attain when dealing with travels and travelers in quantum space.

Chapter Five

With his breath sharply taken away,
P-O ends up on Biosphere K.
Howard has him in tow
And the two of them go
To a strange and exotic display.

Whoosh!!!

P-O gasped "Ooof! That was shattering. My nerves, lungs and senses are well and truly jangled. I have a headache. Why didn't you warn me?"

Howard replied, "You may recall that I did. I strongly suggested that you make the trip under the influence of Morpheus but you would have none of it. Your return voyage is going to be just as trying. It's probably just as well since you now are consciously aware of making the journey to a Multiverse site.

"Where are we?"

"You, my dear friend, are on Biosphere K, an alternate world somewhat like Earth and probably Rhea, if it exists. We are on an exoplanet in a system and galaxy quite different from any you have experienced. Notice the four moons and somewhat cooler sun. This forest is home to the K tribes. We will shortly meet and observe animals that look like us but are not as advanced."

As if on cue, a huge grey-pelted Deer emerged from amid the trees, walked slowly toward Howard and *P-O*, bowed and emitted a series of social grunts. Howard translated: *(Welcome, Porcupine Howard! It has been too long. I have received your request for entry to K. It is granted. Who is your ursine companion?)* The huge buck's antlers were covered in a crown of woven holly branches and berries. Clearly an important personage.

Howard returned the bow and grunted in reply. *(Translation: "Your Majesty. It is good to see you again. This is an associate of mine. I am acquainting him with Multiverse travel with which you are, of course, familiar.)*

The Porcupine turned to the Bear and said, "This is King Capreolinus. He and I have a long history of interaction. I have transported him to Earth on several occasions. He is uncomfortable with our civilization but is willing to accommodate us here in his world. His subjects, especially the priests, reject us Earthlings as abnormal beings but bow to the King's wishes and tolerate us. However, with one or two brave exceptions, they refuse to accompany the King on his infrequent journeys to Earth. As a result, we do not come here that often either. And we are prohibited from taking any actions that will alter their civilization. So be careful."

Howard once more grunted at the Deer, *"(Your Majesty! May we traverse your realm? I wish to acquaint my colleague with your subjects and your habitats, as well as the nature of this planet. He is amazed at your lush vegetation and four moons. As you know, Earth only has one. We shall, as always, pay special attention to your rules of conduct. I hope nothing untoward is happening at this time in your kingdom.")*

The King snorted, stomped and shook his antlers. *("My two sons are acting up again. They are challenging my authority with the help of the priests. They are also threatening the Queen with expulsion. Yours is not a timely visit. I shall have several of my soldiers accompany you on what must be a very short tour. We will start with the Palace.")*

Howard looked at *P-O*. "Are you up for a little royal rebellion?"

"I don't want to precipitate a war. Let's make it a short expedition and go back to your world."

"So, do you now believe there are alternate universes?"

"You could be staging all this but those four moons are a neat trick."

"No trick! You are in another cosmos. When we get back, provided you are convinced that both Rhea and Earth are possible, we will set about finding your own home world. By the way, how many moons does Rhea have?"

"Two, same as Earth."

(Two moons, Hmmm!) "Aha, you admit there may be two different but extremely similar worlds!"

"It's beginning to look that way. Let's not offend the King. I'd like to see his Palace and make a quick expedition through his dominion."

"OK. He's getting a bit impatient. Let's go!"

As they turned toward the forest, several large Bucks carrying pikestaffs fell in beside them. Howard turned toward *P-O* and said, "Part of the Royal Guards. They've been watching us all the time we've been conversing with the King. Note the primitive nature of their weaponry. Firearms are unknown here. They are suspicious of our smartphones but on previous journeys I convinced them they have no dangerous characteristics. I had to disassemble one unit to prove it. They don't know my phone is in contact with UUI. We can communicate across alternate space. *(Courtesy of*

Ursula whose existence was unknown to P-O.) We're approaching the Palace."

The King grunted at the leader of the Guards. Two of the Deer ran forward and opened the heavy oaken gates to a drawbridge that spanned a water-filled moat. Beyond it was a complex of single-story wooden structures. His Majesty turned to Howard and snorted, *("I must leave you here. Affairs of State. It was good to see you again, Porcupine Howard and to meet your ursine friend. We have very few Bears here on K and none as large as he. Captain Blacktail will act as your guide. Leave whenever you wish.")*

After Howard translated for *P-O,* the Bear chuckled. "Well, I guess we're not going to be treated to a royal banquet. Do they have cities?"

"Yes, in a sense. They are more like clusters of large tents behind wooden fences. I'll ask the Captain to show us one. This exoplanet is very small, underdeveloped and lightly populated. We found it by accident. It took us some time to establish relations."

"When we finally convinced the King to make the trip to Earth, he did it in secret. The Captain and two guards came with him. So they won't be surprised when we suddenly disappear. Strangely, for an individual with great courage, intelligence and curiosity, the King has shown no desire to adopt any of our ways or infrastructures. I think he sees that as a path to insurrection. He's probably right. Just as well! Multiverse travel rules: We are constrained from intervening in a civilization's nature unless we are attacked or threatened. I suggest we take a quickie tour of one of their settlements, avoiding the priests if we can and then, if you have gotten more comfortable with the idea of Quantum Travel, we can flash back to Earth and search out Rhea. I want to know how you got to us in the first place."

P-O roared, upsetting the guards. "You're not the only one. Needless to say, I want to get back to my world. I can't imagine what my mate, kids and associates think happened to me. OK, I'm willing to accept alternate worlds exist but I'll be damned if I know how or why I ended up on one, especially your Earth and solar system, a universe that's so similar to my own."

Howard thought for a moment. "That similarity may be part of the reason. We need to give that a lot of thought and investigation. Meanwhile, I think we've arrived at one of the villages."

Captain Blacktail grunted and pointed his pikestaff ahead of us. *("This is Forestgreen. It is one of our Learning Centers. Fawns and juveniles come here for twelve passings of the moons to be taught how to read, communicate and enumerate. The priests also teach them our history and about the gods. They learn about the nature of the forests and the waters. They become acquainted with dangerous animals, places, processes and events. Some of them are selected for special training as healers, food and drink specialists, the military, teachers, priests, courtiers and government members.")*

P-O looked at Howard and said, "Ask him about other species. Where are the Bears and the Porcupines? I haven't seen any Birds. What about Cats?"

"I don't have to ask. I was treated to the history and social structure of the planet on my last few visits. This is my fourth trip. There are other animal groups but deer dominate. The other species are barely tolerated and treated as second class citizens. That is one reason why the priests are highly suspicious of beasts like you and me. Some believe we are anathema – unclean. There are no birds here or any other flying creatures. Cats are regarded as highly dangerous. I doubt if there are more than twenty Bears in this entire world. They don't know about Porcupines."

49

Just then a tent flap opened and a small group of juveniles emerged, led by a teacher or priest. They wore scarves around their necks. They stopped and stared, first at the guards and then at Howard and *P-O*. *("That's a huge Bear, reverend! What's the other animal? Are they prisoners? Will they attack us? Are they unclean?")*

The Captain snorted. *("These are special friends from another world. They are guests of the King.")*

That seemed to stop the fawns and juveniles but not the priest. He snorted back. *("There are no other worlds. The King consorts with tainted beasts. He is not fit to rule us.")*

The Guard stamped on the ground and hissed. *("What is your name, seditious priest? You shall be reported to the Council. You have insulted the King and questioned his judgement and fitness to rule in front of these impressionable young deer. That is intolerable.")*

("You are speaking to a priest of the Great God. I do not take it kindly. Neither will my colleagues. You will stand before the Archpriest and be punished.")

("Keep your idle threats to yourself, superstitious ninny. No one may speak of the King the way you did. Including the Archpriest!")

The students stood horrified. Several of the younger ones sprang around in panic, whining and bleating.

P-O looked at Howard. "This sounds like trouble. Might I recommend we disappear?"

The Porcupine touched a key on his smartphone. "I agree. Hold tight, we're heading back!"

Another whooshing sound. They left the onlookers staring at empty space. *P-O* saw nothing but blackness on the return trip but he certainly felt the quantum impact. Had he felt it before? Yes, of course, on the outbound leg to Biosphere K but maybe before that as well. Curiouser and curiouser. What the Hell is going on?

Chita

Chapter Six

Now you probably all are aware
That dear Juno begot our Great Bear.
She's his mother, you see
And I think you'll agree
That she has a strange story to share.

The Bear's Lair

Octavius had returned to the mansion and was sitting in the Ursine Lounge with most of the Octavians. Belinda, Otto, Condo, the Frau, Chita and I were doing damage to bowls of assorted spirits. The Great Bear, as usual, was amply supplied with mead. The Colonel and Marlin were hooked in at UUI, monitoring the progress *(or lack thereof)* of the two Multiverse travelers. Ursula was on line in both venues. Octavius looked up at the ceiling between gulps of mead.

"I have a thought. *(As Usual!)* Ursula, can you call up my mother?"

"Certainly, Doctor Bear. Audio, video or both?"

"Both please! On the big screen."

Boops, a ring, a buzzing connection, a flashing screen with a logo saying The Home of Juno Bear. A black nose and eyes surrounded by a round sea of pure white fur topped by short pink ears appeared.

"Madam Bear's Residence. This is Florence."

"Florence, this is Doctor Bear. Is my mother available?"

"Oh yes, Doctor. Just one moment and I'll connect you."

A dignified Kodiak sow with a grizzled coat filled the screen.

"Hello Tavi! It's been quite a while. Yes, I know you've been very busy and yes, the electronic deposits are faithfully hitting the bank account every month. Thank you! What's on your fabulous mind?"

"Hello Mom. Are you well?

"As well as an aging sow is entitled to be. A little arthritis and poor Florence has to put up with my complaints. But I'm sure that's not why you're calling. Who's there with you?"

"Most of The Octavians - Belinda, Otto, Condo, the Frau, Chita and Maury."

Hellos all around!

"Mom, I need you to tell us again what happened to you during your famous weird hibernation. By the way, is the gash on your hindquarter all healed?"

"Tavi," cried Juno, "that's nobody else's business. But now that you've blurted it out, it's doing quite well, thank you."

"What gash?" asked Chita. "What happened? Were you attacked?"

"In a manner of speaking! Yes, I was; By a non-sentient bear on an alternate planet."

"Wow. That's weird!"

"All right," said Octavius, "let me give you a little more background. Much against my better judgment, I am involved in a situation that is frustrating and puzzling. We have a Kodiak Bear here who insists he is me."

Juno chuckled, "Is he?"

"No, he is not. It's important for me to check facts and get an opinion, especially from you, Now, Mom, didn't you tell me that while you were hibernating, you felt yourself wake up in a place that was very much like but not exactly your den and its surroundings?"

"Yes, but I'm still not sure I wasn't just dreaming!"

"Fine! Hold that thought. You were by yourself. You searched around for Florence, your Arctic Fox maid, but she was nowhere to be seen. Wasn't that peculiar?"

"Yes, there are times when I wish she'd disappear, but she's always there."

"You went outside, and again, things were almost the same but just almost."

"My den was different both outside and inside, and the woods didn't quite match, but of course, I had been asleep for well over a month."

"But then you saw some other bears, not Kodiaks, and approached them. You tried to talk to them, but they didn't seem to understand. Instead, one growled at you, attacked you and chased you away. That's how you got the gash."

"I ran back to my den, bleeding, and collapsed. I guess I went back to sleep again."

"The next time you woke up, was Florence there?"

"Yes, and everything was familiar again."

"While you were having this experience, did you see any other animals besides the bears?"

"Oh, none I can remember. Maybe a snow rabbit or two. Nobody else."

What do you think happened to you?"

"I don't know. I thought it was a nightmare, but I couldn't explain the gash or the blood. I just didn't know. But, of course, as usual, you said you had a very simple explanation. Megaverse, you called it."

"Multiverse! I may have an explanation, Mom, but it's not all that simple. But, before I do, let me tell all of you about two other stories. The first involves Agrippa."

"You mean your step-brother, Tavi. Come on!?"

"None other, Chita! Don't look so skeptical. I realize Agrippa has a hard time recognizing the truth, much less telling it."

The rest of us had heard this story before. Chita hadn't.

"Where is he, anyway?"

"Vegas or maybe Reno. I'm not sure. You can never really tell where Agrippa is. He claims he was a witness to murder. He was dealing cards in a high stakes poker game when one player accused another of cheating; a fight broke out; shots were fired; one player fell dead; the others ran from the room, leaving Agrippa to sweep up and keep a very substantial pot before disappearing himself. Since then he's been on the run. They, no doubt, want their money back but of course, no one wants to admit to a murder. The police may also be looking for him. I don't know."

Juno spoke up. "I hate to say it, Tavi but I'm not surprised. Yes, I am surprised. Surprised it didn't happen to him years ago. Or maybe it did." She shook her head.

"But Octavius," exclaimed Chita," what has this got do with Juno being attacked by strange bears in a strange world?"

"Just this. The group he was dealing poker for were all *Homo Sapiens*. He says he had been hibernating, woke up or thought he woke up still in Reno. It was another Reno, dominated by h. saps. They didn't seem to find it odd that a talking bear would be dealing for them in a poker game. He said that after the shoot-out he ran with his loot, hid out and eventually fell asleep. When he woke up, he was back in his original den. Everything was the way it had been, except he had a large wad of cash in strange currency that he couldn't account for."

"Tavi, your step-brother's life is one long fairy story. I should know. I'm his mother, although he thinks I'm the Wicked Witch of the West."

Octavius decided to let that pass. "Now, if these two cases of hibernation gone astray were all I had, I wouldn't be so eager to bring it up again. But, one of our Octavians, Wyatt Where, in fact, had been in the military and involved in clandestine security projects before he joined me. One venture was called Project Sleepwalker and was run by General Turmoil and the Business; one of the most secret agencies our government has, or thinks it has. He and a partner had been entering periods of controlled sleep and he's been waking up in other worlds, often populated by h. saps."

"When he surreptitiously left the agency *(No easy task, he thinks his partner was killed to keep him quiet.)* they pursued him for a while, but then they gave up. I suppose they thought he too, was dead or if he was still alive, no one would believe his story. They also thought he couldn't 'transfer' without their help. They were wrong on all three counts. He is very much alive and still making transits for our Multiverse Project with help from Howard

Watt and Marlin. I think this newly arrived Kodiak, *P-O*, is also a hibernating transferee, although probably accidental."

Juno came back. "Oh, Tavi, you do get involved in some crazy things. And…since I seem to have made one of these 'transfers' as you call them, I suppose you want my help."

"Exactly, Mom."

"Well, what the hell, I wasn't doing anything important, anyway. What's next? Where's this Bear's home world?"

"That's the problem. We don't know, and I'm not exactly sure how to find out. We're not even sure it exists. It's certainly not here. The other question is: How many hibernating animals are sharing or have shared the same experience as you or Agrippa? Is *P-O* one of them? If hibernation brings on this transfer process, controlling it is going to be a real problem. Can you imagine bears and other hibernators accidentally taking off at random in multiverse space? Is it happening right now? At the moment, Howard is trying to convince *P-O* that other worlds exist, including his. The Bear says he comes from Rhea, but he thinks this world is it."

"So where is Rhea, actually?"

"Not certain. That's the first thing we intend to find out."

"How can I help?"

"Share your experience with him when he returns from Biosphere K. If I can track down Agrippa, I'm going to enlist him as well."

"Lots of luck with that."

"One possibility. My step-brother has a real talent for running out of ready money and I'm one of his most reliable sources. He's about due for another touch."

"He's a fur-covered sponge. I don't know why you put up with him."

"I can afford it and I don't want him getting killed."

"You're a sap, Tavi but a loveable sap."

"Thanks, Mom, I think. Ursula, do you suppose you could track down Agrippa?"

"I'll try, Doctor Bear but I'd rather do something simple like organize world peace."

"He may be in Reno or Vegas. Try there first. Wave some money around. He'll smell it."

"I'm on it!"

"Thanks! I wonder how our Quantum Wanderers are doing?"

Chapter Seven

Quantum journey's now over and done
And the trip wasn't very much fun.
Was their travel worthwhile
Or a purposeless trial?
Has the real search for Rhea begun?

Simultaneously, alarm bells went off in the UUI laboratory and in the Ursine Lounge at the Bear's Lair. Howard and *P-O* had returned. The Porcupine looked over at the Colonel. who had been controlling re-entry and blew out his cheeks. "Hi Wyatt! No matter how many times I make a Quantum trip, the impact is still the same. Let's check on our ursine friend here."

P-O was sitting on the floor shaking his head. He groaned. "Are we back?"

Howard nodded. "You're in the UUI lab on Earth. Sorry we haven't found Rhea. At least not yet. Octavius and his associates are tied in to us over our network."

The Great Bear's voice boomed out of the lab's speakers. "Welcome back, Mr. Bear. Are you OK? We'll soon find out. I hope your journey was worthwhile. Biosphere K is hardly Earth or, I suppose, Rhea, if we find it but I hope we proved our point. Alternate universes exist."

"I guess I agree. I'm still not sure this isn't Rhea but the evidence seems to be piling up."

"Well, that's a plus. Let's get you checked out. Where's the Doctor?"

Marlin had called for Doctor Bingbang and the Orang bounced through the door, stethoscope at the ready. "OK, Mr. Bear, let's do a quick scan. You too, Howard! Deep Breaths! Respiration-OK; Blood Pressure-In Range; Cardiac-Normal; Vision-Are you near sighted? Hearing-Any buzzes or ringing? No? Try standing! Careful! You got a bruise when you hit the floor! Howard, we have to improve on these landings. Padded room! Yes, yes, I know! Stoat still thinks he's a Nut Case. Alright. Both of you are good to go physically."

Octavius decided to be more gracious now that *P-O* was sounding more reasonable. "Howard, why don't you, the Colonel and Mr. Bear come on over here to the Bear's Lair. We can all have dinner and discuss the situation quietly and sensibly. I have a theory I want to try out and there's someone I want to introduce."

The Porcupine looked over at the Kodiak with raised eyebrows. "Are you good with that?"

P-O nodded. "OK, what the hell. I just want to get this solved. I guess I'll have to trust you folks in order to get that done. This is damned uncomfortable and I must admit I am anxious and frustrated. I want to get back to normal, whatever that means."

Octavius replied, "We share your frustration and understand your anxiety. Let us help. Come on over! Colonel. Find out if Chiti Bingbang and Sigmund Stoat want to join us.

*****

Thirty minutes later, a UUI van pulled up to the entrance of the imposing mansion. A tall Kodiak Bear, Porcupine, Red Wolf, Orangutan and

Stoat piled out and strode, shambled and sidled up to the large entrance portico. Howard opened the door and Octavius welcomed them to the Bear's Lair. The Great Bear and I stood in the huge foyer with a smile on his face and a grin on mine. Scary! Belinda was next to him.

She greeted *P-O.* "Hello! I'm Bearoness Belinda Béarnaise Bruin Bear (nee Black.) Come in, come in! Is this place the same as your home on Rhea?"

"Pretty close. Just enough difference and of course, my mate is not a Polar Sow. She is a Kodiak."

To further highlight the disparities, Arabella and McTavish came bouncing down the main staircase and stood gaping at *P-O.* "He looks like you, Poppa."

"All Kodiaks look alike, kids. This is Mister Bear."

"Hello, young ones! I have four juveniles but none of them look like you."

"We look different because our Momma is a Polar Bear. That's important, you know."

"Yes, I guess it is."

"Where do you come from?"

"A place called Rhea."

"Momma, we've never been to Rhea. Can we go there?"

"I'm afraid not, dear. It's a very long way off."

"How did you get here, Mr. Bear?"

The Kodiak grinned. "That's what I'd like to know."

Octavius interrupted, "That's enough chatter. It'll soon be time for dinner. We'll let Mr. Bear and Howard clean up first after their trip. You too, Doctors and Colonel. Lead the way, Howard, and then join us in the Ursine Lounge for cocktails when you're ready."

Mlle Woof rounded up the Cubs and took them out to the kitchen where Frau Ilse was busy working culinary magic. Samples, samples, samples!

They walked to the lounge where some serious libations were being taken on by the rest of the Octavians *(including Marlin in his tank.)* The Bearoness looked at the Great Bear. *"What's this bright idea of yours, Tavi? Can you get him home?"*

"I'm not sure. First thing we need to do is find Rhea."

"So, you think it really exists. He's not the Nut Case Sigmund Stoat thinks he is."

"Sigmund sees crazies everywhere. No, I believe his story and so does Howard. That exoplanet is out there. Marlin and Ursula are searching as we speak. *P-O* still doesn't know about her and we want to keep it that way. Let's restrict dinner to small talk. I want to call up Mom after we eat."

"What does Juno have to do with it?"

"Hibernation, my dear, hibernation! Neither you nor I go into any kind of winter torpor unless you're pregnant. You're not, are you?"

"No thanks! Once around that track is quite enough, thank you. Two offspring are fine, especially those two! You don't hibernate.

"I adjusted my genes although you say I suffer from narcolepsy. Your levels of nitric acid can hold off the need for deep sleep but Mom does hibernate and you'll recall she took an alternate universe jaunt during one of her sleep sessions. I want her to compare notes with *P-O*. Some champagne?"

"Always!"

Chapter Eight

Dinner time is all over and gone.
And the great search for Rhea is on.
There are planets galore.
Maybe trillions or more.
But just one we are focusing on.

Dinner was wrapping up with loud kudos for Frau Schuylkill's gastronomic wonders. Otto and Chita were exchanging tongue-in-cheek barbs. Condo had *P-O* laughing with his vocal gymnastics. The Cubs were on my case to further promote their electronic games while Belinda and Mlle Woof worked at calming them down. They were ecstatic that Uncle Bruce *(Chief Inspector Wallaroo)* was coming up from Australia on official business in Washington but was stopping by in Cincinnati for a visit.

Chiti and Sigmund were deep in some esoteric medical discussion. The Colonel, Howard and Octavius had risen from the table and were off to the side, exchanging ideas. They got on the line with Marlin for a progress report. Ursula was tied in as well.

The Dolphin said, "I think we may have something. There are several exoplanets in the Alpha Centauri system that we believe have Earth-like characteristics. Thus far they have only been identified by their coordinates and not much has been done by the Working Group on Star Names to lock in nomenclature. Alpha Centauri is 4.37 light years from our sun, fairly close by galactic standards and is actually a triple star system. Let's see if we can get any confirming information from *P-O*."

Octavius turned to Howard. "I think he trusts you. Why don't you ask the questions?"

The Porcupine called *P-O* away from Condo. "We may have a clue here about Rhea but we need some answers from you. Does your planet have a star like our sun?"

"Three in fact, two are bright and close in. One is further out and somewhat dimmer. They're actually a related system. We called them the Triplets. There are other stars in our galaxy but the Triplets dominate. I don't know how you measure time here on Earth but Rhea orbits its star far more quickly than it takes you to go around your sun."

"We are still in guessing mode but we think we may have found Rhea in orbit around the Triplets. We call them the Alpha Centauri system and we know how to get there. It will take some time to determine if a Rhea (Earth-like) planet really exists but we're on it. It may be a disappointment but we're optimistic. Meanwhile, we want to figure out how you got here in the first place."

Octavius took over the conversation. "I assume Rhea has seasons with changing weather and growth characteristics. Earth has four of about even duration: cold Winters; hot Summers; mild intermediate transitional periods-Spring and Fall."

P-O chuckled. "I wish ours was that simple. We have eight.

"Do you hibernate?"

"Do I what?"

"Sleep during the cold periods. *(You know. It's amazing we are speaking the same language – almost.)* Most bears on Earth sleep their way through the Winter. Belinda and I don't. Do you?"

"Yes, of course. In fact, I was just going into my sleep cycle the last time I remember being on Rhea."

"Aha! Good! There's someone I want you to meet. Maury, call Mom!"

I got Florence and Juno on the line. "Mrs. Bear, Octavius wants to talk with you and introduce you to our guest."

Juno appeared on the screen. "OK Tavi, here I am. Introduce me."

"Mr. Bear, meet Mrs. Juno Bear, my mother. The reason I want the two of you to get acquainted is Juno had a fairly recent experience while she was in a state of hibernation. She woke up and found herself in an alternate world, similar but not identical to her home here on Earth. Tell him, Mom."

Juno greeted *P-O* and related her encounter with the non-articulate female Kodiak Bear who attacked her. This was in a spot that looked like but wasn't quite the forest where her den was located. Nursing a gash in her hindquarter, she retreated to the safety of a cave and fell off into unconsciousness. When she woke up, she was back in her own lair with her maid, Florence the Arctic Fox. Florence confirmed the story.

"Now," said Octavius, "my first reaction when I heard your story was to conclude that you and my mother had similar experiences and she had been to Rhea. I no longer believe that since you claim that your world is populated by sentient, socially conscious, self-aware creatures capable of complex thought, sophisticated communication and highly developed organization. Is that correct?"

"You bet! No Kodiak sow on Rhea would have attacked a charming Bear like your mother."

"OK, that leaves us still in the dark about location but I wonder if we can draw any conclusions about process. Both of you were engaged in hibernation. Is it restricted to Kodiak Bears? Do any other creatures on Rhea hibernate?"

"Not many. A few small rodents and a small colony of grizzlies. I've never heard of any of them undergoing your mother's experience. By the way, I'm sure the Bearoness would like to know we don't have Polar Bears."

"Right! So we may, rightly or wrongly, pursue hibernation as a possible trigger for Multiverse travel."

"Maybe, but I wouldn't want to jump to that conclusion."

"No, neither would I, but we don't have much else to go on. Meanwhile, our confidence is building that Rhea exists in Alpha Centauri. Can you provide any input to help that theory along?"

"Well, you've all but convinced me that this world is not Rhea."

"That's progress! I think Howard, Marlin and the Colonel are ready to take a shot at locating your home. We also have Otto who is an accomplished Quantum traveler. We don't want to subject you to another Multiverse jaunt at the moment. Your Biosphere K experience was probably enough punishment. Just relax. We'll be back when our assurance is stronger. Believe me! We don't want you stuck on Earth for any longer than necessary. Do you have any contacts on Rhea that we should be seeking out?"

"Yes, there is my senior vice-president. Oddly enough, she too, is a Porcupine. Her name is Priscilla. She is probably wondering what has become of me. I don't want you pursuing my mate or my family. They'll just panic. Priscilla is a sensible, intelligent animal."

(Maury here) That comment raised an eyebrow or two. Who is this Priscilla and why shouldn't we contact his own family if we find them? Is there something strange going on? I recalled Condo's reactions, calling this guy an earth-bound phony. Could he be right.? The two of them seemed to be getting along with Condo doing his vocal entertainment but that bird is very subtle. We need to talk. I'm standing off by myself at the moment waiting for the Condor and Colonel to break away from the pack and *P-O*. I'd given them the high sign that I wanted to chat with them.

Before they could come over, Ursula rang her chime and I picked up the smartphone. A Lynx looked back at me – today's Ursula image. She changes her appearance as it suits her whim. "Yes, omniscient one?"

"I've located Agrippa. He's on the east coast in Fort Lauderdale. He's working both the casinos and the cruise ships. Right now, he's in a hotel but he's due to ship out tomorrow. He's a dealer in one of the poker suites on the SS Sunbrite. Do you want me to bring him up?"

"Let me call Octavius over. We don't want *P-O* to know you exist."

I waved at the Great Bear and he broke away from the group he was with including *P-O*. I told him Ursula had found Agrippa in Lauderdale.

"Have you got a number for 'Brother Dear'? I'll call him now. Thanks Ursula! Go back to passive mode but record our conversation. I'm more interested in how our Kodiak guest reacts than in what Agrippa will tell him. This Priscilla thing puzzles me. OK! Let's see if I can contact the Florida Gambler."

The Development of Civilization -Volume 12 - Part 4
<u>Alpha Centauri and Planet Rhea</u>
From "An Introduction to Faunapology" by Octavius Bear Ph.D.

We're trying to find Rhea. The odds are against us. Astronomers have estimated that the observable universe has more than 100 billion galaxies. Our own Milky Way is home to around 300 billion stars. Among observable galaxies, they put current estimates of the total stellar population at roughly 70 billion trillion (7×10^{22}). How many exoplanets? Who knows?

Our close neighbor Alpha Centauri is a star 25 trillion miles or over 4.3 light-years from Earth's Sun. It appears as a single point of bright light in our southern sky. It is actually a pair of twin stars (A and B) tightly orbiting each other. A third star, Proxima Centauri, is slightly closer to Earth and is much smaller and dimmer.

A lucky shot! A planet seems to be orbiting one of the twins, Alpha Centauri B, every 3.24 days. It is possibly just a bit bigger than Earth, orbiting in a "habitable" zone. We believe the planet could be Rhea, home of our newly-arrived Ursine, P-O. Ursula has traversed the distance through a wormhole and examined the nature of the planet. Her report follows:

"Envision an exoplanet, Earth-like in size but orbiting at extremely high speeds around its star Alpha Centauri B. It has two moons and the star Alpha Centauri A is clearly visible as well. It has large bodies of water and volcanic islands with little in the way of habitable space. Nevertheless, there is a remarkably close resemblance to our Earth, not just physically, but in the nature of its civilization. For this putative Rhea is populated by a relatively small number of species closely akin to our own. Their overall

numbers are miniscule. Homo Sapiens does not exist there. It is not clear they ever did."

"I have been able to identify equines, ursines, felines and other mammalian species similar to those on Earth. There are no reptiles, fish, insects or birds. The inhabitants are mentally capable and self-aware. Most of them speak and write a single language not unlike English with a few dialects. Technologically, they are behind Earth although some seem to understand space and extra-planetary travel. Several groups including Admiral Tumult and his Company are convinced other worlds exist in far-away systems and galaxies. Most Rheans think that is a myth."

"Their civil structure is highly militaristic, hierarchical and centralized in several large urban areas. Submission to authority is paramount. Diversity of thought is not tolerated. I could not detect any religions. Males dominate but some females have ascended to positions of power."

"The exoplanet is running out of space for its population. The Admiral believes that in a relatively short time period it will be necessary to migrate from this planet to other worlds to provide "living room" for the growing number of inhabitants. Hence, his interest in Multiverse travel."

"Further exploration on our part is certainly called for."

Chapter Nine

The Octavians have to speak out.
On P-O they all have lots of doubt.
Is he wearing a mask?
Who's Priscilla? they ask.
Hey, just what is this guy all about?

The Colonel, Condo and I headed off to a separate conference room. I waved at Otto to come on and join us. He was in the middle of a conversation about multiverse travel and he shrugged in our direction. Howard, Marlin, Chita, Belinda, Octavius and *P-O* were caught up in some technical fine points of quantum transfer and the Frau had just come on board. Octavius had taken out his oversize smart phone and dialed the number in Florida. Buzz, buzz!

"You have reached the number of Sir Agrippa Bear, international specialist in games of chance. I am not currently available but am most interested in hearing from you. Please leave your name and a number at which I can make contact and I shall return your call forthwith. Thanks awfully."

"Agrippa, this is Octavius,. You've moved your location and changed your cell number. I wonder why. Ha!! Cut the phony Brit routine and call me back as soon as you get this. You know the sequence. The one you use when your finances are on the rocks."

He hung up. He looked at *P-O*. "I'll send for you when he calls back. I want him to share his hibernation travel experience or experiences. Meanwhile, I'll leave you in the paws of this charming company. Come, Otto." He headed off toward our conference room leaving the merry band behind looking at him quizzically.

*****

The Condor and Colonel had just settled into two comfortable leather chairs and I had jumped up and perched on the conference table. I was about to start the conversation when the door opened and the Great Bear strode in with Otto. "Don't let me interrupt, Maury. *(Yeah sure!)* I'm very interested in what is bothering you gentlebeasts. Do you think our guest has a hidden agenda? Have a seat, Otto."

The Colonel spoke up. "We're not sure, Octavius but something doesn't smell right. Why doesn't he want us to contact his family and who is this Priscilla Porcupine? Is she some girlfriend he wants to keep hidden. Is he running some kind of conspiracy involving you and UUI? Who is this Admiral Tumult? Is *P-O* and this Priscilla working for him? We really should have Howard in here with us. What happened at Biosphere K?"

"Wow, Wyatt, that's quite a litany! What do you others think?"

I piped up. "His story and his reactions have holes in them. Is there really a Rhea? If there is, first he makes it out to be Earth but then it's not Earth. Does he really want to leave here? What's he up to? I don't trust him."

The Condor concurred, "It doesn't hold water. You know, I wonder if he really wants to go back to this possibly mythical Rhea. He may have escaped his home planet for some reason, overplayed his hand with us and doesn't know how to work his way out. He could even be an escaped criminal who knows damn well what multiverse travel is all about."

Octavius scratched his head and no doubt, would have welcomed a beaker of mead. There was none forthcoming. "Otto, see if you can get Howard in here without raising our friend's suspicions. If you need to, tell him we are having a security issue at one of the UUI plants and this group is responsible. It's weak but it will have to do. By the way, don't let the twins get near him. They'll blab everything they can think of although they might get some interesting facts from him. Nah, let's keep them apart!"

"Ursula, what do you think?"

"Doctor Bear, I've been filtering and correlating my statistical algorithms and I tend to agree with this group. There's something wrong. Perhaps we should accelerate our search for Rhea and when we find it, just dump him back on it."

The Colonel howled. "I guess I'm the paranoid in this pack but I'm not comfortable with just letting him go back, wherever back is, with a stock of information about us, UUI, Earth and Multiverse Travel. Suppose he is working for this Admiral Tumult, if he exists. He could be dangerous. I think we should isolate him."

Octavius issued one of his famous "Hmms."

Just then Howard opened the door. "Well, this a serious group. What's up? By the way, Bruce Wallaroo just arrived."

Chapter Ten

The arrival of Bruce Wallaroo
Adds a really great mind to our crew.
He's a highly skilled cop
But his jumping won't stop
And he plays on a didgeridoo.

Chief Inspector Bruce Wallaroo from Down Under requires no introduction to crime aficionados. He has bounded his way through forests of felonies since he first emerged from joey-hood and is now one of the world's leading criminologists – on a par – although Octavius would never admit it – with the Great Bear himself.

His career began as an obscure foot patrolman in Melbourne – bouncing along on his beat in the seamier parts of town – The Bounding Bobby, they called him. There weren't many marsupials on the force and even among them, he stood out, if for no other reason than his inability to stand or sit still. He came dangerously close on several occasions to being mustered out by his superiors for being too energetic.

After rescuing the Mayor's daughter from a pack of wild dingoes one night, he was promoted to Sergeant in the plain clothes detective division. And thus it began. It turned out Bruce Wallaroo was a very fine, nay excellent, detective and he became a legend in his own mind. Promotion followed promotion as he cracked thefts, robberies, murders, drive-by embezzlements, art and jewel heists. He was called on by Interpol and began to spend more of his time on international assignments, now as a representative of the Australian Federal Police. He began undercover work, but discovered he hopped around too much to keep the covers on.

It was on one such assignment – an international peat moss smuggling ring – that he met Octavius Bear. Together, they caught the chief smuggler, a nasty Irish terrier, broke up the ring, got peat moss prices down once more to reasonable levels, and saved the industry from being shoveled under.

So, Wallaroo sprang up from Aussie obscurity and bounced to the very pinnacle of his profession. Together, he and Octavius have created legends that are studied worldwide in police colleges, intelligence training programs and even detective correspondence courses.

Yes, Inspector Wallaroo is a marsupial of the highest intelligence but he is also virtually unintelligible with his heavy Strine accent. *(By the way, Reader! I am translating his Strine to understandable English for you. No thanks required.)*

He can also reduce a room to rubble by the simple act of "pacing back and forth" – which in his case consists of springing from one vertical or horizontal surface to another with incredible speed and impact while his Aussie mind moves at warp nine.

Needless to say, we never allow Frau Schuylkill and Wallaroo to be alone in the same room. She would no doubt tear him apart in a moment, all the time snarling about his "big dirty feet all over my nice clean sofa." or "*Ach*, another broken end-table." Right then, I could hear her howling loudly in the kitchen – her standard reaction whenever Inspector Bruce Wallaroo arrives.

And don't let Bruce at the controls of a helicopter. He flies one the way he moves. Swoops, jumps, bounces, nose dives, drops, plunges, skids, sideswipes while tossing in a stomach churning collection of near misses with objects, vehicles, structures and individuals. Needless to say, the Cubs adore him and keep pestering him for a ride in a chopper. Belinda, a highly skilled fixed and rotary wing pilot herself, won't hear of it.

In any event, here he was fresh from an assignment in Washington DC and was making what he thought would be a social call.

"G'day all! This looks like some kind of solemn conclave. What's going on?"

Before anyone could answer, the Cubs descended on him. "Hi, Uncle Bruce. Did you come in a helicopter? Can we fly with you?"

"Sorry, young 'uns! I flew commercial and snatched a car ride over from CVG Airport."

"Aww, Gee! Well anyway, say Hello to Mr. Bear. He's from a different planet."

Belinda to the rescue. "I'll do the introductions, kids. Thank you."

Bruce looked at the Bearoness and then *P-O*. "G'day, Bruce Wallaroo. Glad to meetcha."

P-O stared at the marsupial, shook his paw and asked, "Are you an Australian policeman?"

"Too right! An old friend of Ocko, the Bearoness and all the crew. Known 'em for years."

Belinda interrupted. "This needs a little explanation, Bruce. Why don't you stow your gear, grab yourself a beer or two and I'll fetch Tavi. He's in the next room. *(P-O doesn't know the Inspector, she thought. That's interesting.)*"

She walked over to the conference room and knocked on the door. Octavius answered. "Bruce is here," she said.

"So Howard just told us. OK, why don't we put this discussion on hold while I bring the Chief Inspector up to speed on the situation. I want to hear from everybody and I'd like him to be part of the conversation. Maury, has Agrippa called back?"

"Not yet!"

"He mustn't be desperate for cash or he's already on the ship."

"Want me to call again?"

"No, let's wait a bit. I want to handle this event first."

Belinda said, "*P-O* doesn't know Bruce. Isn't he supposed to be you?"

Octavius nodded, "I think we're about to dispose of that little ploy. Ask him to come on in to the conference room. Howard, What's your take?"

"Well, clearly he isn't you. I do think he's from an alternate world. I'm not sure whether he deliberately or accidentally transferred to Earth but this act he's trying to pull off has gone sour. Let's face him down."

Chapter Eleven

Now, here is an unpleasant fact.
P-O's carrying out a fake act.
And the brains of the plot
Is Agrippa, what rot!
The Great Bear is too shocked to react

A knock on the door. "Come in, Mister Bear. Have a seat. First off, what is your real name and where are you from. Your story so far hasn't convinced anybody as I'm sure you know. So what's your game?"

P-O's first reaction was to try and brazen it out but common sense took over. "OK, bad call on my part. My real name is Otis Bear but I really am from Rhea. The planet exists. I'm an actor by profession. Not a very good one, it seems."

"Who put you up to this? I don't believe you planned this all out without some help and coaching. Why the act in the first place. What do you want?"

"I'm on a fact finding mission for Admiral Tumult and the Company. Yes, there is an Admiral Tumult. You guys have cornered the market on Quantum Transfer and he wants your know-how. First he thought of making a deal with General Turmoil and the Company but they didn't want to play. So, the Admiral decided to target you and your staff. He knew you wouldn't work with him, either. My job is to capture Howard and get him to Rhea where we can pick his brain. By the way, Biosphere K was not my first alternate world journey. But it was the easiest. Our techniques are primitive by comparison. They seldom work."

"Someone helped to plot this all out. Where did you get all your knowledge of UUI, the Octavians and me?"

"How's your sense of humor, Octavius?"

"I'm not very tolerant when kidnapping is involved. Is someone on my staff a traitor?"

"Yes and No!"

"I'm warning you, Otis. I'm in no mood. You've created a lot of bother and expense and I'm not taking kindly to it."

"Oh, alright! You ready? It's your stepbrother, Agrippa. He's been very well paid for coaching me and the Admiral's staff."

The Great Bear was thunderstruck. "The bastard. *(Narrator's note: He actually is!)* No wonder he's not answering his phone and is taking off on a ship! He'd normally do just about anything for a healthy fee."

I looked at Octavius. He was livid. I wondered what Juno would do when she heard about it. Agrippa was never high on her Santa Claus list. This would put the icing on the cake.

The phone rang. Agrippa was on the line. Talk about chutzpah. "Tavi old sport. Understand you're trying to reach me."

"Count yourself lucky I can't reach you. You'd be a bearskin rug."

"Why, whatever has got your spleen hyped up, old boy? Careful. You're not getting any younger. Doesn't pay to get upset.

"I have just had an interesting discussion with Otis Bear of Rhea, _old boy_! He has told me about your dealings with Admiral Tumult and your assistance in their plot to kidnap Howard."

"Kidnap Howard!? What nonsense! I was just giving the Admiral the benefit of my knowledge and experience with you and your minions. They have an interest in your work in Quantum Motion and admire your progress."

"Cut the BS, Agrippa! First of all, you can write me off as your perpetual piggy bank. No more money from this hoard. Wait till Juno hears about this. I'm sure you'd rather deal with me. Second, stay the hell away from me and my people unless we call for you. They all have a commission to knock your block off on sight. Third, if you don't want to be hunted down forever, you'd better come up with a plausible report on what the Admiral's up to and I mean right away. I am going to dump your buddy Otis back on Rhea. Oh, yes, we found Rhea and I am coming after you and them. Don't think that cruise ship is going to protect you."

"Alright, Tavi. You've made yourself quite clear. No need to track me down. I shall appear at your luxurious digs in four days. This is a short cruise devoted to gambling. I have commitments."

"I should come out there and haul your ass back here immediately. If I get any indication that you are still working for Admiral Tumult, you're toast. Meanwhile, I have Otis, your actor friend, to contend with and he's on his way back to Rhea forthwith. You've gone too far this time, Agrippa. I hope that ship sinks and you with it."

"Thank you for your gracious wishes, Brother Dear. I'll see you in four days. Say hello to Otis for me."

Maury Meerkat

Chapter Twelve

Long discussion on moving ahead
But events will take over instead.
Should they take steps today
To send P-O away?
It won't happen since Otis is dead.

Breakfast was proceeding apace in the dining room. Octavius was holding court with Howard, Marlin, Condo, the Colonel, Otto, Frau Ilse, Chita, Belinda, Bruce and me in attendance. The Cubs and Mlle Woof were off at another table and the Flying Tigers had finished their meal and were on their way to the hangar to supervise aeronautical maintenance tasks.

"No, Howard, you are not going to Rhea. Not with a threat of kidnapping hanging over your spiny head. Are you sure of Rhea's location? Can't we just take hold of Otis and return him, wrapped up in pink ribbons, to the Admiral? Where is Otis, by the way? Get him, will you, Maury. We need to talk. He's going back. We just need to discuss how."

I stuffed down the last vestiges of my breakfast and left for the bedroom wing where we had housed Otis yesterday evening. As I reached the second floor, I was intercepted by Doris, one of the Labrador chambermaids.

"Oh, Mr. Meerkat, I was just running to get you. It's that Mr. Otis, the Kodiak Bear. He's lying on the floor in his room and I can't wake him. I think he might be dead!" She snuffled and tugged on my arm.

"OK, Doris, let's go look. When did you find him?"

"Just a few minutes ago. His was my next room to tidy up. Oh. I do hope he's not dead."

Unfortunately, her wish was not going to come true. I took one look at the large fur-covered body and grabbed the phone. "Get me Dr. Bingbang! Chiti, come over to the Bear's Lair as fast as you can. It's Otis. You know, Pseudo Octavius. I'm pretty sure he's dead. Cause or causes unknown. No violence that I can see but I haven't touched the body. I'm calling Octavius and the Colonel. We may have to call the police if you say so. "

"Octavius? It's Maury. I'm up in Otis' room. He's stretched out on the floor. I'm pretty sure he's dead. The maid found his body. Chiti's on his way over. Yeah, You and the Colonel. It could be natural causes. I don't know. I don't think we have to call the police yet. Bring Bruce with you. A member of law enforcement can always help even if he's from Australia. I'll wait here for the doctor."

Doris, why don't you take a break. We'll call you if we need you. Good girl. Sorry you had to see this."

"He's not my first dead body, Mr. Meerkat. but thank you."

*****

Octavius left the dining room and signaled for Colonel Where to join him. "Wyatt, we have a situation. Maury just called down from the bedroom wing. Looks like Otis is dead. The maid found him when she went to do up his room. Doctor Bingbang is on his was over to confirm it. Not sure if it's natural causes or foul play. Come on. Bring Bruce! Ursula, get on this!"

"Yes, Doctor Bear!"

"Bruce, we have a mysterious death on our paws. Otis, our Multiverse traveler. We were going to send him back to his world today. Now we'll have to investigate and determine what happened before we can. We have Doctor

84

Bingbang on his way but if we have to call the police, we could use some help from you. I'm not delighted with having to explain parallel universes and how he got here to the constabulary. I'm still not sure how he did get here."

"Gotcha, Ocko. He's a foreigner. International incident. Interpol and all that. I'll take charge. But among us, we do need to find out what happened."

"You bet and to help us, here comes the Orangutan. Doctor Bingbang, thanks for coming so rapidly."

"No problem. Where is the body?"

"Here in this bedroom. The chambermaid found him about an hour ago. He has not been touched. Maury is convinced he's dead but we need your say-so."

"Let's take a look. Can we turn him over. He's huge."

So is Octavius. With a little help from Bruce, the Colonel and me, Bingbang and the Great Bear got Otis over on his back. The Orang prodded and checked for vital signs.

"Oh, he's dead all right. No signs of life. No signs of violence either. My first reaction would be heart attack or some other natural cause. Can we move him down to your mansion's medical room? Do we have any history on him?"

"No, but I think I can get some information while you run your tests. Let me know if we have to contact the local police. Chief Inspector Wallaroo is here. Maybe you and he can satisfy them. And the Colonel is a good friend of our local Police Chief and Coroner. I'd like to keep them out of this, if we can. Explaining Multiverse is never easy, especially in the case of a death."

"Ursula, get a hold of Agrippa. He may already be on that cruise ship. Very important we speak to him immediately. Don't take 'no' for an answer. He knows he's in trouble already. His cooperation will help him."

Two of the house staff brought up a gurney from the medical room, strapped the huge body in and took it down to the basement level. In spite of the restraints, it hung over the edges and showed signs of falling off several times. Doctor Bingbang got ready to perform his tests. I returned to the dining room where breakfast was still progressing in earnest and passed on the news to the as yet uninformed members of the team."

Belinda reacted first. "Do we know how he died, Maury? Is there a possibility of foul play? Who saw him last?"

"I'm not sure, Bearoness. He knew we intended to send him back to Rhea today. Howard and Marlin had located the planet."

Howard piped up. "We found the planet but we don't have exact coordinates. Octavius put the kibosh on my making a trip there since the Admiral was intent on capturing me and picking my brain to enhance their Multiverse efforts."

Otto looked up from his plate. "I'm the selected traveler. As you know, I can zap around the landscape and avoid being caught. Howard can't. Are we still going to send me to reconnoiter."

"That's up to Octavius. Right now, he and Ursula are tracking down Agrippa, the fink."

Chapter Thirteen

Otis' death has sure left us in doubt.
What was all his playacting about?
Did that bear have to die?
Does Agrippa know why?
Now the whole nasty story comes out.

The Great Bear's smartphone rang simultaneously with Ursula's chime. She had tracked Agrippa down and he was on the line. "I say, Octavius, I'm in the middle of dealing a very serious game of Texas Hold 'Em. Can't this wait?"

"No, it can't. Your buddy Otis is dead!"

"What? How?"

"We don't know yet. The doctor is still examining his body. It may be natural causes but we can't be sure. I need some answers and I need them now."

"Oh, God. I was afraid of this."

"What does that mean, brother dear?"

"The damned fool was trying to play fast and loose with you as well as the Admiral and the Company. Not conducive to good health."

"Explain!"

"Rhea and the Company do exist and Admiral Tumult wants Alpha Centauri to dominate the alternate universe. He tried to enlist General Turmoil and the Business to form a joint enterprise for cosmic conquest. Negotiations failed. I don't know how Otis found out the Zebra wanted to take over the

Multiverse world. You are acknowledged as the Prime Mover in Alternate World travel. He's an actor who looks like you. He convinced the Admiral that he could substitute for Octavius Bear if they could kidnap you and take you out of circulation. Otis and I go back to early days of mutual alternate world travel. I was hired to provide a convincing background to give credence to his claim of being Octavius Bear. They were going to force you to give up your secrets. Failing that, they were going to capture Howard."

"Otis decided to embellish the scenario and play both ends against the middle. He wanted to try to take over UUI here on Earth. He is (was) a talented actor but not much on planning and execution. Too many loose ends. It clearly didn't work."

"No, it didn't and you are clearly a target for the Rheans. If they killed Otis, you're probably next. I'm tempted to just let you hang out there, you creep. Meanwhile we have an ursine body to examine and dispose of. Do you know who his next of kin are and how to locate them."

"There aren't any. Did he tell you he was married and had cubs and juveniles?"

"He did!"

"Not so! A play for sympathy. He was a loner. *(and a liar)*"

"That explains why he didn't want us making family contact although he told us he was assisted by a Porcupine named Priscilla."

"Oh, she exists. She's the Admiral's Executive Officer. Most of this plot was her brainchild. Otis worked for her. I think she was fascinated by Howard and wanted to reel him in."

"Sorry to disappoint her and the Admiral. I've never had to deal with a Zebra, especially an angry striped equine intent on conquering the universe. Do you have the coordinates we can use to ship the body back?"

"Not specific. I can give you the general vicinity but you'll have to search it out. Don't send Howard!"

An exchange of cosmic geography took place.

"Agrippa, you're worse than I thought. I don't know how or why Otis died but you have clearly betrayed me, my family and associates, your family and the Earth in general. Rhea may have killed Otis. We don't know yet. If I hear that you have warned the Admiral or this Priscilla, you can consider yourself totally written off. If you want my protection, I can send a helicopter to get you off that cruise ship. Plead serious sickness. You've got a half hour to make up your mind. Ursula will be monitoring you."

"Maury, Ursula, Colonel. Call the group together. We need to make Otis disappear!"

*****

Later, Belinda, Howard, Wyatt, Bruce, Chita, Condo, Frau Ilse, Otto and Marlin slowly joined the four of us in the large conference room. Ursula had also asked Doctor Bingbang to attend as well and he bounced into the room.

"I'm not finished yet, Octavius, but so far it looks like natural causes to me. Heart Failure."

"That's fine Chiti. I don't want to be covering up a murder. If we can keep the police out of it, that's great. Cuts down on lengthy and hard to believe explanations. When you do finish, can you write up a death certificate? Don't use your real name. I want to attach it to the body when we ship it back to Admiral Tumult in Rhea"

He proceeded to relate Agrippa's sorry tail. Several votes for killing Agrippa. "Never did like that Bear. Hang him out to dry."

Octavius just shrugged. "Ursula, have we heard from him yet."

"Just now, Doctor Bear. He's coming. I chartered a helicopter to pick him up from the cruise ship. The Flying Tigers are ready to transfer him up here on the Concorde."

Belinda looked up. "Do you know where to ship Otis' body?"

"Not exactly. We'll get the rough coordinates from Agrippa. Now I want Otto, our stealth agent, to zap to Rhea, lock into the exact location of the Admiral's Company and guide the shipment. For goodness sake, Otto, don't get caught."

"You know me better than that, Chief."

Condo asked, "Why are we doing this? Why not just quietly and surreptitiously bury him somewhere. In spite of his claims, didn't you say he had no connections to anyone here on Earth? Except, of course, Agrippa."

"A warning. I want to tell the Admiral and this Priscilla we're on to them and not to try another half-baked stunt like that one."

"They're going to think we killed him! This could start a war!"

"That's why I want the death certificate. Natural Causes. Of course, they may not believe it but they can have their physicians do a post mortem. We'll see. Get ready to go, Otto!"

The Development of Civilization -Volume 12 -Part 5
Hairy Otter and Psycho/Telekinesis
From "An Introduction to Faunapology" by Octavius Bear Ph.D.

Although often spoken of as interchangeable capabilities, psychokinesis (PK) and telekinesis are somewhat different. Psychokinesis involves the mental impact on physical systems and objects without the use of any physical energy. For example, the famous mind-induced bending spoon. Telekinesis refers to the <u>movement</u> of physical objects or individuals by purely cerebral force. The physical object in question may even be the individual who is exerting the force, creating an act of mind-based self-propulsion. In a sense, telekinesis is a subset of psychokinesis.

There seems to be no consistent relationship with telepathy. As noted elsewhere, some animals have developed telepathic means of communication as a result of the Big Shock. Few, if any, telepaths have telekinetic abilities.

Psychokinetic and telekinetic talents are rare and not very well understood and the few known paranormal practitioners are frequently accused of fraud. We have a telekinetic specialist on our team of Octavians – Hairy Otter or as we refer to him, Otto the Magnificent. Otto is something of a mystery to us and to himself but a fraud, he is not. Too many witnesses can swear to his abilities and some have suffered mightily as a consequence of not taking him seriously. How threatening can a silly river otter be?

His talent seems to be the result of genetic manipulation by the evil and now very deceased Imperius Drake – a mad duck intent on world revenge and conquest. He sought to turn Otto into his highly capable slave but only succeeded in creating a telekinetic adept. Otto is not a telepath.

The otter is not always in complete control of his capabilities. It seems a burst of adrenaline is necessary to trigger his talents. Fortunately, his existence is replete with adrenaline raising situations. He is a sparkling entertainer adding hilarity to the shows put on by the Bearoness' Aquabears. He has been in high theatrical demand, providing comic relief to the precision balletic routines presented by the Polar danseuses.

However, he is also a formidable physical opponent in combat situations and has been known to overwhelm his foes by exercising his ability to send them reeling and collapsing without touching them. Perhaps his most useful talent is his capacity for concealment and escape. Now you see him. Now you don't. He refers to this activity as "zapping."

He is also capable of rapid local, interplanetary and intergalactic Quantum transit and is a highly skilled Multiverse traveler. His primary mission to Rhea is to find the Admiral and Priscilla without being discovered, and via Ursula, guide the delivery of Otis' corpse to their doorstep without them being any the wiser how it got there. With the assistance and control of our other Alternate Planet specialists here on earth - Howard Watt, Colonel Where and Marlin the Dolphin, Otto's trip to Rhea should be swift and successful. At least that's what we hope.

Otto the Magnificent

Chapter Fourteen

Looks like Otto's on Rhea, alright.
In the Admiral's office at night.
But his "zappings" enroute
Cause the Zebra to shoot
And Priscilla's caught up in the fight.

Next morning's breakfast was interrupted by the sound of jet engines whining in the courtyard near the hangar. The Flying Tigers had transferred Agrippa from the chartered helicopter at Fort Lauderdale and had flown him up on the Aquabear SST. Record time. Good show, cats!

Otto smiled. "This is what I've been waiting for. Agrippa has the detailed location of the Admiral's facilities. He'd better be playing it straight."

Juno had joined us by an Ursula linkup and was ready to tear into her stepson. "I can't believe he'd do something that sleazy. Well, yes, maybe I do. He's a disgrace to Kodiaks."

Octavius chuckled. "Mom, wait till he gives us the information we need before tearing his head off. Here he comes now."

Agrippa came into the room. His limp was more pronounced than usual. Surprise! "I say, Bearoness, That is a wonderful aircraft. First time I've been on it."

Belinda snorted, "And probably the last time as well. You're not very welcome, you know."

A major understatement. You would need an ice scraper to cut through the frost in the room.

Octavius growled. "This is not a social call, Agrippa. We want to hear what the Admiral has in mind in detail and what led up to this cockeyed scheme."

"I told you on the phone. Admiral Tumult is intent on making Rhea the center for advanced Multiverse conquest. His first step is to dominate Alpha Centauri but that's only the beginning. He knows that you and your team are the intergalactic authorities on Alternate Worlds. He also knows that Howard and Marlin are the leading experts with help from the Colonel."

"How does he know all this unless you've been selling him the information?"

Silence!

"How did they know about you?"

"I've known Otis since the first time I made a journey. He was dealing cards, too."

"Where? Was it Rhea? You have been on Rhea a number of times."

"I never did learn the name of the planet where I first met him but it wasn't Rhea. That came later."

"Are there Homo Sapiens on Rhea?"

"I don't think so. I've never seen any."

"You say the Admiral and Priscilla know about Howard, Marlin and the Colonel. Do they know about Otto?"

"No, Otis thought Otto was simply a show-business clown and passed over him in his reports to Priscilla and the Admiral."

"Have you enlightened them?

"Hell, no. I'm in enough trouble as it is."

"You better be telling the truth. If something happens to our lutrine associate while he's on Rhea, you're going to wish you were dead. But I'll leave you alive to suffer after Mom gets through with you."

More Silence!

"Tell us about Priscilla!"

"As I told you, she's the Admiral's Executive Officer. She's extremely ambitious. This whole thing with Otis was her idea. He worked for her on special projects. She didn't account for Otis having his own private agenda on Earth. She's fascinated by Howard. She believes Porcupines are intellectually superior animals and she's out to prove that she can even outstrip Howard's talents. She is more dangerous than the Admiral who is enough of a threat as it is."

"She overegged her pudding, though. Not as clever as she thinks she is. Otto, when you dump Otis' body make sure both Priscilla and the Admiral are there. I don't want her scrambling out of the hole she dug for herself. OK! Let's get those coordinates and send Otto on his way. Otto, don't take any crazy chances. Ursula, are you sure you can track and assist him?"

"I've been to Rhea already, Doctor Bear. We're cool. We'll get him placed and then send the body. Agrippa, give us the detailed coordinates for the Admiral's offices."

*****

"OK, Your Magnificence, ready when you are!" Howard's voice crackled over Otto's smartphone which also was carrying a version of Ursula.

"I'm good to go, Howard. Just don't dump me in a sewer."

"Why not? You can just do your Telekinesis thing and zap out of there."

"Yeah, but not before I got all wet."

"But you're a river otter. You should be used to it."

"Yeah, yeah! Oops!!"

A whoosh and Otto the Magnificent, aka Hairy Otter, found himself sitting under a tree in a small green, dimly-lit park. It was across the street from two formidable granite structures surrounded by a tall wrought iron fence topped off by barbed wire. A cluster of antennas and a helipad were perched on the roofs. No signs or flags. Only a windsock for the helicopters. A spot-lit guardhouse stood next to a single enclosed driveway that led around the buildings, probably to a parking lot, underground garage or both. Two armed and uniformed animals that looked like coyotes were also doing their best to look menacing. They were succeeding. A military vehicle with numeric markings – no names, no initials - sat off to the side.

The otter looked up at the grey evening sky. What are the probables? Sure enough, two moons looking down at the planetary landscape. Just a sliver of starlight. This was probably Rhea and the compound was probably the Company. OK. Time for a little zapping and querying. First, let's report back to the Bear's Lair.

97

This was going to take a little bit of time to overcome the distance and possible radiation interference. "Hey, Howard, I got here, I think. Ursula seems to be on track. Agrippa's coordinates look right. I'm not going to rush in without doing a bit of reconnoitering. Back to you soon."

"Let's start with the garage," he thought. "Less likely this time of night to run into anyone who'd be suspicious of me. I can work my way to the executive level and scout out exit paths in the process. Now, which of the two buildings?"

He zapped and found himself in a crowded garage crouched behind a military truck with a horse trailer attached. A circle of five stars on the doors and starred flags on the front fenders. Best guess – the Admiral's vehicle. Sure enough, a sign painted on the floor. "Reserved for Admiral Tumult." Well, he's still in residence. Interesting. The sign and other symbols were in English or what looked like it – elevator; stairs; numbered parking slots. A cosmic coincidence? Wow! We thought Otis was faking it. They really do speak English here. What are the odds on that?"

Ursula responded. "Twelve million, four hundred thousand, two hundred thirty six to one."

"Thanks, Miss know-it-all! Any thoughts on our next move?"

'Hold on. I just heard from Howard. Shall I confirm our location?"

"Yeah, tell him it's evening. The building seems right. We're in the garage. Next stop – the offices. Top floor."

He bounced out in a storeroom that also held several power generators. "Stupid me. This is a military facility. Executive offices are probably underground somewhere. Let's give the elevator a try."

He summoned the car and when it arrived he looked at the access buttons. The lowest two were controlled by electronic key locks. One level was probably for the computers and communications gear although they may be in the other building. In fact below the parking level, it looked like the separate buildings were actually combined into one big space. The other button seemed to be for Executive Row and the top brass. Which one? Nothing for it but to give one floor a shot. Speaking of "shot' let's hope he didn't end up zapping into the business end of a weapons toting coyote. OK, down the shaft and out!

A long corridor and…offices! Bingo! Executive country. Since it was evening, most of the departments were dark except for several at the very end of the corridor. Admiral Land? Let's go peek. A large desk and several flags sat in the middle of the corridor in front of a corner office. No doubt a receptionist/guard occupied it during working hours, whatever they were.

Otto crept along the corridor ready to zap away at a second's notice. Voices! Equine speech and a series of high pitched porcupine squeaks in response. The Admiral and Priscilla.

The Zebra brayed, "Why haven't we heard from Otis? He's overdue to report in."

Priscilla replied. "I don't know. He's usually quite reliable. He came back from a trip to Biosphere K with Howard Watt and was preparing to capture the porcupine and bring him to us. Those naive Earth-dwellers thought he turned up in their world by accident. Otis had to make the journey to the Biosphere in order to keep up appearances. We haven't heard from Octavius' half-brother Agrippa, either."

"Well, follow up immediately. Howard Watt is vital to my plans to conquer the Multiverse. I want that quilled genius in our custody now. I want to know why only certain species can engage in Quantum travel. I'm not one of them. Why am I not able to transport? Our scientists are a bunch of incompetents. It's a shame I had to dispose of several of them to inspire the rest."

"On the other hoof, Priscilla, all you Hystricidae seem to be gifted with great intelligence. Your idea of sending Otis to Earth to pretend he was Octavius and capture Watt was a masterstroke. But it's not complete! Bring Otis back with his hostages! Snatch Octavius Bear but we need Watt. Get him here. Now! I will not tolerate failure. You are valuable, Priscilla and I wouldn't want you and Otis to share our scientists' fate. But you could if you botch this. Do I make myself clear?"

"Very clear, sir. You can rely on me. I'll have them here shortly."

Otto whispered to Ursula. "Let's give her a hand. Get Howard and Marlin ready to send off Otis' body and dump it in the Admiral's office. I'm going to pop in there and grab Priscilla, spines and all. We'll take her back to Earth as a prisoner. We need to know what the Admiral's up to. Let me know when our geniuses are set up."

The AGI said, "Listen for my chime."

Otto zapped into the executive suite and appeared atop a file cabinet. "Greetings Admiral! Hello Priscilla!"

"Who the hell are you and how did you get in here? Priscilla, call the guards." The Zebra reached into a drawer and pulled out a pistol.

Otto ducked under a table. "Now Admiral, let's not get trigger happy. My name's not important. I have a package for you special delivery from Earth."

Ursula rang her chime and Otis' body crashed onto the floor in front of the Admiral's desk. On reflex, the Zebra fired his gun, missing both the body and Otto who was now behind a chair.

The Otter squeaked, "Yes, that's Otis or what was Otis. He's dead! We didn't kill him. He died of a heart attack. You can read the death certificate attached to his collar." Otto was back on top of the file cabinet. "Priscilla, sorry your little scheme didn't work. Howard Watt is safe at the Bear's Lair on Earth. Would you like to meet him?"

A guard ran in. The Admiral shouted. "Grab and hold that Otter. Priscilla, this is your doing. Hold her too."

Otto dove down and landed next to the table. Priscilla lunged at him and managed to grasp his paw. He shouted, "Ursula, Now!"

A whoosh and the two of them disappeared, leaving both the guard and the Admiral staring goggle-eyed at empty space. "Where did they go?"

After a short plunge into darkness, the porcupine learned the answer to that question. Still holding onto Otto's wrist, she tumbled head first on the floor of a well-lit laboratory. Four faces stared down at her. A very large Bear, a Wolf, a Meerkat and a male Porcupine.

The Bear snorted. "Priscilla, Welcome to Earth. I'm Octavius Bear."

Admiral Tumult

Chapter Fifteen

Major Colin Coyote appears.
What's the frantic confusion he hears?
The Admiral's wild.
Is Priscilla exiled?
Things are nastier than his worst fears.

"Find them, you fools. Don't let that Otter escape. How did he get in here in the first place? Who is responsible for such a security lapse? I could have been killed. Major, I want the names of the idiots who let him get past our barriers. They are dead meat."

A coyote wearing a plain black uniform decorated with two gold leaves tried fruitlessly to break in on the tirade. "Sir, none of our alarms went off. He got past all of our detectors. They have always been foolproof. You designed them yourself."

That undiplomatic remark just further inflamed the Zebra's wrath.

"And someone subverted them. Who? Priscilla!! Where is Priscilla? I want answers. Find her but don't kill her. I reserve that to myself. You, Guard! Get this body out of here! No, wait! Call in the Medical Officer. I want to know how Otis died!"

All Hell was breaking loose at the Company on Rhea and the Admiral was causing most of the breakage. An assassination attempt! He had been threatened by an Otter, no less. A whiskered clown! Intolerable! He was totally flummoxed by Otto's telekinetic stunts. His first reaction was that Otto and Priscilla were in cahoots. She was an ambitious traitor who wanted his job. She would be swiftly, summarily and fatally dealt with when she was caught.

As would the Otter. Little did he know he would have to reach across multiple light years of space to make that happen. In spite of his leadership of the Company, it didn't occur to him that Multiverse action was in play. Tunnel vision! Quantum Tunnel Vision!

The Medical Officer had been called from his bed and was supervising the removal of Otis' body. He read and re-read the death certificate attached to the Bear's collar. It had been written by an unknown doctor in an unknown place called Kentucky. Where was that? Somewhere on Rhea, no doubt, but where? Heart Failure? Perhaps. There were no signs of physical violence and without extensive testing he could not pinpoint any poisons. He needed to see the Bear's medical history. Meanwhile, the Zebra was getting close to having his own heart attack.

"Does that fool doctor know what he's doing?" *(Then the penny dropped.)* "Aha! Otis was on Earth. They murdered him. Any idiot can see that. Octavius Bear! He killed Otis. Who was this ridiculous Otter? We thought we knew all of Octavius' minions. Did he come from Earth or was he an assassin hired here on Rhea? How did he get the body? How did he get it into my office? Otis never mentioned him. Priscilla may have been keeping him a secret. Oh, she's going to suffer!"

The Admiral was jealously aware that only Priscilla, Otis and a few scientists were capable of traversing the Multiverse. Among the Rhean species, equines and most others lacked the ability and knowledge needed to journey to alternate worlds. Bears and Porcupines could. Perhaps Otters could as well. He wanted that Otter.

"Major, bring in all the Otters in Rhea for questioning. I don't care how many there are. Just bring them."

"But, Sir, there are hundreds." The Security Commander was convinced that the Zebra was going off the deep end. He wanted to confer with the Medical Officer. Did Otis die of natural causes? If so, how to convince the Admiral to shelve his paranoia about assassination. Not going to happen at this moment. Just grin and bear it *(no pun intended!)*

The Admiral waved his pistol. "Bring them in, you incompetent, or would you prefer to meet Otis' fate?"

"Yes sir! Of course!"

"Don't just stand there. Organize your coyotes. Sweep the city! Cover the country, They can't have gotten far. I want them here! Now! I will not be threatened."

Ironic coming from the Zebra! Yet another threat and another order that would be conveniently forgotten or delayed. The Coyote needed to reach Priscilla and warn her *(and the Otter for that matter)* that the Admiral was out for her quill-covered hide. But where the Hell are they?"

Priscilla

Chapter Sixteen

Ms. Priscilla has run out of luck.
She's on Earth and she seems to be stuck.
That red wolf sure sounds tough.
Things may soon get quite rough.
She needs all her brainpower and pluck.

Otto extricated himself from Priscilla's death grip on his wrist. "Hi Gang! Here I am. Back again unharmed. I delivered the body direct to the Admiral. He's not happy. I brought a guest back with me. Meet Priscilla. I don't think she's very happy about being here although she did want to meet Howard and snatch him back to Rhea. Well, here he is, ma'am! Unfortunately for you, the trigger happy Admiral thinks you're a traitor. So you have two uncomfortable choices. Us or the Zebra!"

The porcupine shook her head that was still ringing from her impact with the floor. She looked from Otto to Octavius to Howard and Marlin's screen. She stared quizzically at me. Then she peered at the Wolf.

The Colonel snarled at her. "I'm Wyatt Where in charge of Octavius Bear's security. For the moment, you're not going anywhere except a cell. You're also not getting your claws on Howard. We know you put Otis up to that charade. Not too smart. Too many loose ends. Just so you know, he did die of a heart attack. Your doctor on Rhea has his work cut out for him. I'm sure the Admiral is not well and truly pleased."

Howard looked at her closely but said nothing. Very attractive and no doubt, highly intelligent and knowledgeable. Also quite dangerous. Careful, careful!

Octavius raised his eyebrows, such as they were. "You know, the ironic thing is we located Rhea anyway although Otis knew where it was all the time. He was playing your game. We were ready to ship him back to you alive when he had his heart attack. So, we sent his body with our extremely clever Otto in charge. We wanted you and the Admiral to know we were on to your game. I hope the Zebra isn't going to try something stupid like trying to attack us. I understand he's a bit of a hot head. I wouldn't want to give odds on your longevity if you try to go back there."

She finally spoke. "You may be right. I don't know what he's going to do. Do you still have Otis' belongings? He had a communicator we used to keep in touch. If you'll let me use it, I can call a friendly officer on Rhea and find out what's happening. "

The Colonel howled, "You have to be kidding!"

The Great Bear reacted, "No, Wyatt, wait. Let's think about this. Priscilla, who is this friendly officer?"

"Major Colin Coyote, Director of Security for the Company. He's in trouble with the Admiral for letting Otto here slip past our barriers. He probably knows where I am."

Wyatt looked at the Bear in wonderment. "You're going to let her contact their Security Chief? C'mon Octavius! Get serious!"

"No, *I'm* going to contact their Security Chief. Maury, Do we still have Otis' communicator?"

"I'll check. We didn't ship any of his effects back with his body."

"See if you can find it. We don't want to use you-know-who. That's our secret!"

Priscilla stared at him and shook her head in puzzlement.

Of course, he was referring to Ursula who was taking all this in in passive mode. She had travelled back and forth with Otto via his smartphone. She had previously done her recon mission on Rhea, gathering location data, demographics and intelligence about the Admiral, Priscilla and the Company. When we left the room in search of Otis' communicator, I called up the AGI.

"Ursie, we're alone. We don't want the Porcupine to know you exist. So, let's you and I discuss the situation while we're out of the room. What do you think? I don't think we can trust Priscilla but right now, she's in a pickle and may be willing to cooperate. Should Octavius contact this Security guy? He may be able to shed some light on what the Admiral is going to do."

"I think Doctor Bear is astute enough to handle her and this Major. The Admiral is another nut case and is likely to be unpredictable. The more we can learn about him, the better. For some reason, his species can't Quantum Travel. At least not yet and at the rate he seems to be killing off his scientists, he probably won't in the near future. It's not clear who and which Rheans can traverse Quantum Space. What we need to know is how many and how loyal his followers are. Maybe we can precipitate a backlash. He's certainly a tyrant. Strange! Zebras are usually calm and peace-loving creatures."

"So, you're casting one well thought out vote for Octavius contacting the Security Chief."

"Yes, now let's see if we can find that communicator."

*****

"Alright, Priscilla, we're looking for the device. Maury Meerkat is my sidekick or executive officer, like you. While you're here, you'll be dealing with him as well as Howard and the Colonel. By the way, we are not military. Colonel Where has long since retired but he can make Quantum journeys. One of my nemeses here on Earth is General Turmoil and his Business – not unlike your boss and his organization. I think you know them. I believe the Admiral was trying to team up with him. No Sale as I heard. While we're waiting for Maury, tell us some more about Rhea. What is the government like? How important is the Admiral?"

She replied. "Rhea is a planet roughly the size of Earth. A Pan-Rhean Council governs the globe. Equines are the dominant members. Our world is mostly water, ice and uninhabitable volcanic land. We don't have enough useful room for our population, small though it is. That's one of the major reasons we are looking to migrate by Multiverse Transfer. We have several potential targets. Earth is one of them. That makes the Admiral's Company one of the most influential entities on Rhea. He was a member of the Council.."

"He is a despot and has his own military auxiliary to do his bidding. He has ambitions to take over the Triumvirate. He is paranoid but like most of his kind he has true enemies. He will not hesitate to dispose of anyone he believes is opposing, failing or threatening him. I suppose, in spite of my loyalty, I am now in that category. That's why I want to talk to Major Coyote. I need to know what my status is. Look, your Meerkat Executive is returning."

I came back into the room with Otis' communicator in paw. An Ursula had been surreptitiously recording Priscilla's statements and would play them back for me later. Right now, Octavius had to make up his mind whether to let her reach out to the Admiral's Security Chief.

Chapter Seventeen

The Octavians all are quite wary.
Her tale could be imaginary.
Credibility's small.
They don't trust her at all!
They think caution is most necessary.

While she had been talking, a side conversation was going on among the Octavians in the room. Condo seemed to be leading the discussion. He looked at Priscilla and then Octavius and said, "The consensus is don't let her communicate with Rhea. They can probably backtrack the communication and pinpoint us. We don't trust her. Her story may be pure fantasy or deliberate lies. She might set off an attack or worse."

The Porcupine fired back. "Look! I'm in deep doo-doo and the Major, if he's still alive, is probably in worse shape than I am. He and his team let Otto get through his security and then let us escape. The Admiral is hardly thrilled."

Otto piped up. "Just a second, Priscilla. You were following the Admiral's orders. You were trying to hold on to me and got dragged along when I zapped and then transferred back to Earth. You're an accidental fugitive. You can't switch loyalties just like that."

"I can when my life is on the line. OK, There's no reason why you should believe me. Here, Octavius, you guys must be smart enough to block a trace. I'll give you the contact numbers for Major Coyote. You call him. If he's under arrest, they may have taken away his communicator. Tell him whatever you want. I just need to know my status and his."

I looked at the Great Bear. "I think you should know your anonymous advisor *(Ursula)* thinks you should make the call. If the Major is available and playing it straight, we may be able to find out what that crazy Zebra has in mind."

The Porcupine peered at me, no doubt trying to figure out who this 'anonymous advisor' was. She probably thought it was me being cute. Let her!

"Well, what are you going to do?"

The Bear snorted, "I probably should take the Colonel's advice and toss you in a cell, if we had one. OK, in spite of all the objections, I'll make the call. Give me the device and the numbers."

Several minutes went by with hisses and background noise. The Great Bear allowed Priscilla to listen in but not to speak except through him. Finally, a high pitched howl and a growl. "Yes? Who is it?"

Octavius growled back. "Is this Major Colin Coyote, Chief of Security for the Company?"

"It could be. Who is this? What are you doing using that confidential communicator."

The Great Bear replied. "My identity is unimportant. What matters is we have Priscilla Porcupine, the Admiral's Executive here as an unwilling guest. We are using Otis' communicator to contact you. We are not permitting her to speak with you directly. We will relay her questions and comments, as appropriate. May I suggest you respond fully and truthfully."

"What is going on? Is she a prisoner?"

"In a sense, yes! You should know we are aware of the Rhean scheme to infiltrate us with the late and unlamented Otis."

"Aha! So you are Earthlings!"

"No comment. Ms. Porcupine wants to know what the situation is with the Admiral. She believes she may be in danger."

A pawse. Then, "She is. The Admiral believes she is a traitor and he can't be convinced otherwise. He thinks she is in cahoots with that crazy Otter. He has put out an all points search for both of them. He has commanded me to bring in every Otter on Rhea for questioning. There are hundreds. It will take my staff weeks to gather them all in. I am dragging my feet on that order but I can only do that for so long before I fall under suspicion."

"Are you saying you are opposed to the Admiral?"

"I'm not going to admit to that. It's worth my life."

Octavius looked at the Porcupine. "It doesn't sound particularly safe for you on Rhea."

She shrugged. "Ask him if Otis really did die of natural causes."

The Bear relayed the question.

The Coyote barked. "The Medical Examiner agreed with the Death Certificate attached to Otis' body. That earned him a trip to the cells. The Admiral is convinced it was all part of an assassination plot against him by Earth and Otis was murdered as part of it. What is Priscilla's condition there with you? Sounds like she's a prisoner."

A sharp look by The Bear at the Porcupine. "We haven't decided on that yet. A lot depends on her."

"Well, tell her to stay away from Rhea until I give her the 'all-clear.' I'm not sure of my own situation. If it's OK with you, have her call me every few days. If you can't reach me, I'm probably under arrest or dead. By the way, who are you?"

"Somebody interested in Multiverse Travel. No names."

"Is that Otter one of your people?"

"Yes, you won't find him on Rhea. The Admiral is in for a big disappointment."

"Well, in the interest of preserving my hide, I'll keep looking for him anyway but slowly."

The Porcupine interrupted. "Is the Council aware of what is going on?"

Octavius passed the question on. The Major laughed. "The Admiral has them all bulldozed. They're concerned about assassinations, too. Don't expect any help there."

The Bear looked at her. "Are we finished with the Major?"

"Yes, for the moment. Tell him to keep in touch." Octavius signed off..

"Alright, milady, we have to have a long, straightforward discussion. You don't have to fear for your life unless you try something stupid. We're going to confine you to a comfortable room, feed you and explore possibilities. We seem to be your only choice since we have no intention of sending you back to Rhea. You may want to make some proposals of your own. Threats or bribery will not go down very well. And don't try reaching out to General Turmoil here on Earth. We have him blocked. I'll have Frau Schuylkill take you in paw. She's a great cook but also a deadly shot. See you later."

Frau Schuylkill

Chapter Nineteen

The Coyote is now on the spot
For the Zebra is making things hot.
He has choices to weigh.
He decides he will play
With Priscilla and Otto. Why not?

"Well Major, Have you tracked down that crazy Otter yet and where is the treacherous Priscilla? Must I remind you again, I will not tolerate failure. My tolerance is at a low ebb. Your time is almost up."

In the sterile silence of the dimly lit executive corridor, the Admiral's darkened office was even more ominous than usual and so was the Admiral. The Zebra was clearly obsessed with striking down his apparent assassins at any cost – that is, any cost to his opponents.

"My officers are sweeping the country, sir. They have a number of Otters in paw but none of them fit the description of that telekinetic pest. He is quite unique."

"I don't care how unique he is. I want him alive and I want him to lead us to Priscilla. Tell your staff they are not kill him. I don't care if he's roughed up. In fact, all the better to get him to talk. But I want him to be able to talk. After I get what I want from him, you may kill him or perhaps I will. Is that understood?"

The Major knew he had to act to stop the Admiral. He needed to talk with Priscilla. But she had to initiate the call.

*****

116

"OK, Maury, Colonel and Ursula. We've all heard Priscilla's conversation with Howard. What are your thoughts? Here comes Howard. Join us. Is she intent on overthrowing the Zebra? She's a very sharp and smooth character. Is she just playacting to get a shot at returning to Rhea and taking over the Company?"

Howard spoke. "She can't go back until the Admiral is out of the picture. I don't know. She's plausible but then a number of charlatans make their living being plausible. She may want to take over the Company after he's gone and be as bad, if not worse, than he is."

"What do you think, Maury?"

"Sorry, I'm not in the Priscilla camp but what are our choices? We don't want to hold onto her forever or release her here on Earth. I think we help get her back to Rhea and keep a very careful watch on the Company if it continues to exist, especially with her in charge."

"Colonel?"

"I agree with Maury but I'm not enthusiastic."

"Ursula?"

"Let her talk with the Major. We can closely monitor it. They may try to communicate with members of the Council and convince them to get rid of the Admiral. If she's successful, it's what she does afterward that can be troublesome. Although she has a rational view of Rhea's inability to take over Earth, we don't know what she would intend for other planets. Rhea is pressed for space and resources to support their overpopulation."

"OK, let's give her the communicator and let her talk to the Major. Maury, call her down and tell her what we're going to do. Don't tell her about our doubts. Ursula, as usual, monitor passively."

*****

"Hello, Priscilla. I'm Maury Meerkat, Octavius Bear's sidekick. Howard is tied up at the moment and I have been elected to bring you down to our meeting room, give you the communicator and help you contact your associate on Rhea. Is that Major Coyote?"

"Hello Maury. You're cute. We don't have Meerkats on Rhea. Are you a rare species? You're not really a Cat, are you? And yes, my associate is Major Coyote, the Admiral's Chief of Security."

"No, Meerkats are pretty common here on Earth. We're no relation to Cats. Of course, I am pretty exceptional. *(chuckle)*"

"You're Octavius Bear's associate. What a contrast! He's huge and you're so small. I hope he never sits on you."

"Only verbally. We get along quite well. Speaking of strange relationships -You're a co-conspirator with the Admiral's Chief of Security? How does that work out?"

"I wouldn't use that conspiracy term. We're both loyal Rheans. It's just that the Admiral has become more paranoid, dangerous and dictatorial lately. We think he needs to be replaced."

"By whom?"

"Not by me or the Major, if that's what you're thinking. Actually, we think the Company ought to be shut down and a new Scientific Agency created in its place."

"With you at its helm?"

"No, I see myself as an advisor to the Council. Female chief executives are very rare on Rhea."

"Come along with me and you can tell us about the Council before we set you up to talk with the Major."

They left her rooms and took the elevator to the basement floor and a conference room where Octavius, the Colonel, Otto, Condo, Belinda, Chita, the Frau and Bruce Wallaroo were gathered. Howard was there as well and Marlin was hooked up as usual.

"Well," she said, "this is quite a congregation. Am I on trial?"

"Not at all" said the Great Bear. "We all want to hear your description of the Rhean Council; any further comments you want to make about the Admiral, his supporters and his intentions and then, I'm afraid we plan to eavesdrop on your conversation with the Major. Sorry, no privacy at the moment."

"I guess I should have anticipated that. Let's get it over with. Alright, Rhea in a nutshell: The planet has seven geographic city-states. The largest is called Prime. It's the seat of planetary government. Home of the Council. It's where your Otter landed. The Company is located there. Each city-state has an elected representative on the Council. A triumvirate is a sort of steering committee. All told, there are fifteen Council members, all males. Most, but not all are equine. In addition to the seven city-state representatives, eight more

119

are functional specialists - finance; military *(including the Company)*; health and welfare; security and justice; science and education; transport; agriculture; business. The Admiral shares authority with the military Council Member, a good friend of his. Some even consider them a sort of shadow government even though the Triumvirate is in overall charge. The Council Chairbeast, who is the real Chief Executive, rotates every three years among the city-state members. The current Council member for Prime City is my Uncle Portnoy. A Porcupine. He is a former Chairbeast and quite influential."

"That's how I got my job. You may think that would keep me safe from the Admiral but no such luck. If he can prove that I am guilty of treason and have instigated an assassination attempt on him, not only will I be in jeopardy, so will my Uncle. I have to reach Uncle Portnoy or more to the point, I have to reach the Major who will have to reach him. I don't know whether the Admiral has already denounced me. If he has, we'll have to protect Portnoy from his Council enemies."

"The Admiral is not well liked but he is feared. He has, literally, been getting away with murder. I think there are enough Council votes to unseat and exile him but we need to be sure. That's why I need to talk to the Major. Both of us are convinced that the Zebra wants to overthrow the Triumvirate and the Council, rule Rhea as a dictator and proceed with his plans to take over the entire Alpha Centauri system. If he can master Quantum Travel, he intends to then invade another physically hospitable exoplanet like Earth and go on to rule the cosmos. He has to be stopped."

"And yet," said the Colonel, "you were willing to assist and abet the Admiral's plans until you were captured. Why should we believe you?"

"Because when you work for the Admiral, you don't have a choice. His way or no way. I was too much of a coward to defy him but now that my life is on the line, I don't have much choice, do I? I need to talk to Major Coyote and get our message to the Council. They have to be made aware of his plans to overthrow them. Supreme irony. He's accusing me of treachery while he hatches his own plots. Do I get the communicator?"

Octavius looked around the room. Sensing no further questions or objections, he handed the communicator to Priscilla. "Howard, get her connected. Rhea's day-night cycle is much shorter than ours. Will the Major be available?"

The Porcupine looked at a watch-like device on her front paw and nodded. "He should be up."

Howard with Marlin's help, activated the phone and guided it across the Quantum regions.

Buzzes and rings. a high pitched howl and a growl. "Yes!?"

"Major Coyote? Someone wishes to speak with you. Is your line secure?"

"Yes! Is that someone Priscilla Porcupine?"

"Hello, Colin. It's me. I'm OK. These Earthlings have decided to let me talk with you. Are you alright?"

"So far, but I'm not too optimistic for my future. The Zebra is getting very impatient. He wants you and the Otter in confinement or preferably dead. He believes you're both still hidden away on Rhea. I haven't enlightened him.

I have spoken to your Uncle Portnoy and I think I have him convinced that the Admiral is plotting against the Triumvirate and the Council."

"Portnoy is meeting with the Council members who usually support him. They are a majority including the current Chairbeast. Several are military veterans who have put down revolutions in the past. But support is not unanimous. Two delegates are perpetual fence-sitters. I'm charged by the Chairbeast to gather evidence of the intended coup and report back tomorrow. I think I have enough to blow the whistle. Meanwhile, stay where you are. Your Uncle wants you out of harm's way."

Priscilla winced. "I don't think I'm going anywhere any time soon." She hung up.

Octavius yawned and fell over. His narcolepsy had kicked in. The Porcupine was shocked. "What's the matter with him?"

Belinda to the rescue. "He's narcoleptic. It's a long story. Nothing to be concerned about. The episodes are usually quite brief and we make sure he doesn't come to any harm while he's under. He'll be back shortly and not even remember he was out. Meanwhile, if we can overcome his snores, let's continue the discussion. Can the Admiral be safely exiled, preferably away from his supporters?"

"There is a chain of islands that we use for sequestering dangerous criminals. We'd have to select his jailors very carefully. I think the Triumvirate would prefer to have him executed."

"That sounds pretty bloodthirsty."

"So is he. I don't know how many scientists, security guards and others he has disposed of. I need to talk with Major Coyote again. The Council minus the Admiral should have met by now. We'll see how persuasive Uncle Portnoy has been."

Belinda turned to Howard and told him to power up the communicator. After a few minutes, the Coyote was back on the line.

"It's a tie as of the moment. With the Admiral not voting the fourteen member Council is evenly split. I don't think they're going to get another chance to vote. The Admiral has learned about Portnoy's complaint and is setting his coup in motion. I'm going to make myself scarce."

Belinda looked over at Otto. "I think a little Multiverse travel and Telekinetic action is appropriate. Does the Admiral know your skills?"

"Not all of them. I think I can make him disappear. Tell me about those islands, Priscilla. Where are they?"

"Wait, the Major can get you the coordinates."

"Better be quick, Major. We have some Rheans to rescue and a trip to plan for the Admiral. I'll meet you outside the Company's Headquarters in a short time. I'll be your prisoner." He and Howard went into the labs.

A groan, snort and rumble. Octavius was coming around.

When he awoke, Belinda told the Great Bear what was happening. He thought for a moment and then signed off. Priscilla was watching all this wide-eyed. "What is this skill Otto has?"

"He's telekinetic. Not only can he zap from place to place, he can move others and objects just by thinking it. He does a wonderful comedy act but this time he's deadly serious."

"Can he drop the Admiral on one of the detention islands?"

"I think so and he can get the Admiral's prisoners released."

"That's amazing...and useful."

"Don't even think about it, lady. As you already know and the Admiral is about to find out, Otto is formidable. Some folks have found that out the hard way"

"Otto, are you ready for another Quantum trip?"

"As soon as I get the detention island coordinates. Will the Admiral be safely imprisoned there?"

The Porcupine twisted her nose and luxuriant whiskers. "His jailors will be loyal to Portnoy and the Major. Oddly enough, several of them were consigned to the islands by the Admiral as a punishment. It's almost as bad as being a prisoner. They can't get off until they've served out their time. The Zebra is certainly not popular with them. OK, Otto. Here are the numbers. The Major will be waiting for you. Good luck!"

"Look out Admiral, Here I come!" Whoosh!

Chapter Twenty

The mission is moving ahead,
Otto's teamed with the Major instead.
There's a new number two,
Colonel Barbicon, who
Makes an early departure, shot dead.

Rhea-Prime City-The Company: It was early evening again and Otto was back in that same park opposite the Company's Headquarters. He shook his head several times to clear his vision. The same military vehicle was sitting in the driveway and the guardhouse was populated not by two but three coyotes in uniform. The third was the Major. He and one of the guards advanced on the Otter with weapons extended and said, "Paws up! You are a prisoner of The Company's Security Force."

Otto squeaked and tried to get away. The guard grabbed him and knocked him down.

"Alright, Sergeant, let's take him into the building. The Admiral is very eager to get his hooves on this character."

"Why, Major? He looks pretty harmless."

"Appearances can be very deceiving. We've been rounding up Otters all over the planet just looking for this guy. Now we've found him. OK, you can return to the guardhouse. I'll take him from here." He yanked Otto's shoulder and pushed him ahead through the door and into the basement. "C'mon. You have an appointment."

The door slammed and the Major looked up and down the corridor before he turned back to Otto. "Sorry about the rough stuff. Good acting on your part!"

"I've had worse pummeling. Do you have the coordinates? Is the Admiral in his office."

"Yes to both. The Zebra has a new Executive Officer, a Badger. Colonel Barbicon. He's a former military officer. I'm pretty certain he's been put in charge of organizing the coup against the Council. Dangerous animal. I'm going to bring you down to the Admiral's office. Be careful. You know how trigger happy he is. I don't know about this new Exec."

The Otter shrugged. "We'll see. Hey, satisfy my curiosity. What is he an Admiral of?"

"Rhea has a small Navy, mostly for coastal security. The Admiral was Chief Naval Science Officer until he convinced the Council that an organization like the Company was necessary. He held onto the title."

"So he's never been involved in warfare?"

"Not him! The only weapon he has ever used is his sidearm. You know about that."

"He's a lousy shot. I don't suppose you know much about this new Exec."

"I'm assuming he knows how to use a weapon. So do I.

"Let's hope it doesn't get to that. So the Admiral needs support organizing a coup. I didn't think he'd trust anyone. Did he trust Priscilla?"

"He was pretty ready to call her a traitor. I doubt if he trusts me."

"Well, let's get to it. Any last thoughts? Oh, by the way. Who's on the island we're sending him to?"

"A couple of homicidal maniacs. OK, you're my prisoner again."

They moved into an elevator and the Major used his badge to activate the car downward. They stepped out into the empty executive corridor. The only light was coming from the Admiral's rooms.

"Doesn't he ever sleep?"

"Yes, standing up in his office. Has his meals sent in. He has his own private lavatory."

"Not much for social life! OK! Show time!"

The Major pushed and shoved the Otter who proceeded to shout and curse.

The Zebra called out. "What's going on out there?"

"It's Major Coyote, sir. I have the Otter."

"Is he secured? Bring him in. Aha! So, my prickly faced adversary, we meet again. What has he told you, Major?"

"Nothing helpful, sir. Just piling on abuse."

"Let him go, Major. *(Wrong Move!)* Alright, Mr. Otter, where is Priscilla?

"Who?"

"Oh, we're going to play games. Colonel Barbicon, come in here…armed."

The badger waddled into the room, holding a mean looking weapon. He looked at the Major, sneered and then looked at Otto. "Is this the troublemaker?"

"Yes, and he's not being cooperative. Persuade him to answer my questions."

He held the barrel end of his pistol and swung the butt at Otto who was no longer standing in front of the desk.

"Where is he?"

"Here, brush puss!" Otto was under a table. The badger rushed at him. Major Coyote moved to one side of the room. The Admiral took his pistol out of his desk drawer, fired twice at Otto and hit the Exec. *(The Zebra was a lousy shot!)*

The Otter took advantage of the chaos and said, "Enough of this nonsense", stared briefly at the Admiral and watched him disappear.

The Major went to look at Colonel Barbicon, held a paw in front of the badger's mouth, shook his head and said, "He's had it."

He reached for the phone. "This is Major Coyote. Send the doctor and a couple of guards down to the Admiral's office. Colonel Barbicon has been shot. I believe he's dead. The Admiral has disappeared. Call the national police."

He turned to Otto. "I think you'd better disappear, too."

"OK, Ursula, let's skedaddle." Zap!!

Epilogue

Now it's time to tie up some loose ends.
Are the Porcupines really just friends?"
With the Admiral gone,
Will a romance turn on?
I will coyly just say, "It depends."

The Bear's Lair: 1 week later:

The Octavians plus Priscilla had gathered in the underground conference room to talk with Major Coyote on Rhea. He was relating the situation at the Company since the Colonel was killed, the Admiral had disappeared and Otto had left the scene. Otto sat munching on a plate of fish cakes from the Frau's kitchen.

Octavius was leading the discussion. "So the police believe the Admiral shot and killed Colonel Barbicon."

"Correct. It seems the bullets that killed the Badger came from the Admiral's gun that they found lying on the floor. I helped things along by reporting that the Admiral was having a fierce argument with his Exec over something. It is common knowledge that the Admiral was a terrible hot head."

"How did you explain the missing Otter?"

"It was commonly understood that the Admiral had authorized a sweep of all the Otters on Rhea. The guards who had seen Otto couldn't distinguish him from any of the other suspects. Just another Otter! He probably faded into the group that was released from the cells after the Zebra disappeared." Otto chuckled and murmured "Zap!".

"The Company has been dismantled by the Council and will be replaced by a Pan Rhea Science Center dedicated to peaceful exploration and development. Councilbeast Portnoy wants his niece, Priscilla to run it. The Triumvirate has agreed. Now, all we need is the return of Priscilla who seems to be in hiding somewhere on Rhea. *(wink, wink)"*

A mystery. An unidentified body of a Zebra has been discovered on one of the penitentiary islands in the frozen ocean. No solid clues yet.

*****

Howard and Priscilla were sitting in the Ursine Lounge working over bowls of champagne celebrating her return to Rhea and her new assignment.

"Well, Howard. I'm certainly happy about the way things turned out and I swear to you there will be no invasion plans underway on Rhea. The Company is no more. The Council is convinced the Admiral was an insane despot and all traces of his rule are being erased. I'm looking forward to my new assignment but I am disappointed that you won't join me. We could be very happy. I need a Chief Scientist and I could dearly use a mate."

"I'm sorry, Priscilla. The prospects are very tempting but I'm too dedicated to the Octavians and the Great Bear at this point in my life. We have so much to do in the Multiverse. We can keep contact. I know how to reach Rhea and in spite of your pretense that you were hiding away on your planet, you know how to reach me. We can keep up a Quantum affair."

<h2 style="text-align:center">THE END</h2>

The Casebooks of Octavius Bear - Volume 12

<h1 style="text-align:center">The Nut Case</h1>

About the Author

Harry DeMaio is a *nom de plume* of Harry B. DeMaio, successful author of several books on Information Security and Business Networks as well as the twelve-volume *Casebooks of Octavius Bear for MX Publishing.* He is also a published author for Belanger Books and the MX Sherlock Holmes series edited by David Marcum. A retired business executive, former consultant, information security specialist, pilot, disk jockey and graduate school adjunct professor, he whiles away his time traveling and writing preposterous books, articles and stories.

He has appeared on many radio and TV shows and is an accomplished, frequent public speaker.

Former New York City natives, he and his extremely patient and helpful wife, Virginia, and their late lamented and much loved Bichon Frisé, Woof, live in Cincinnati (and several other parallel universes.) They have two sons, living in Scottsdale, Arizona and Cortlandt Manor, New York, both of whom are quite successful and quite normal, thus putting the lie to the theory that insanity is hereditary.

His e-mail is hdemaio@zoomtown.com

You can also find him on Facebook.

His website is www.octaviusbearslair.com

His books are available on Amazon, Barnes and Noble, directly from MX Publishing and at other fine bookstores.

www.ingramcontent.com/pod-product-compliance
Lightning Source LLC
Chambersburg PA
CBHW080816250626
47159CB00010B/3404